Cheers for Robert Campbell and the First Jake Hatch Mystery, *PLUGGED NICKEL* . . .

"And the Campbells keep coming, hurrah. . . . Campbell does a bang-up job with Hatch, who is smart and quick and honest, and who has a lady friend in every small town on the route. Campbell creates an old-fashioned mystery, with clues and red herrings and all the apparatus, while also bringing to life the small-town ways that some of us once knew well before society found itself hip-deep in people. . . . Jake Hatch is fine company."

—*Boston Globe*

"*Plugged Nickel* is a good one. . . . The main attraction is the wonderful cast of ordinary but unique people. Campbell's characters have that true ring of authenticity that distinguishes fine crystal from window glass."

—*Cincinnati Post*

"Campbell is a heckuva storyteller; *Plugged Nickel* clickety-clacks along the tracks like a Burlington-Northern freight train."

—*Criminal Record*

"An infectious tale. . . . A nostalgic run from small town to small town, as Hatch breaks down [illegible]spects with his homespun patter and fierce de[illegible]ion. . . . This series is a winner."

—[illegible]geles, CA)

Look [illegible]ystery:

Ava[illegible]ket Books

Books by Robert Campbell

Alice in La-La Land
Plugged Nickel
Red Cent

Published by POCKET BOOKS

RED CENT

Robert Campbell

POCKET BOOKS
New York London Toronto Sydney Tokyo

This book is a work of fiction. Names, characters, places and incidents are either the product of the author's imagination or are used fictitiously. Any resemblance to actual events or locales or persons, living or dead, is entirely coincidental.

An *Original* Publication of POCKET BOOKS

POCKET BOOKS, a division of Simon & Schuster Inc.
1230 Avenue of the Americas, New York, NY 10020

ISBN: 0-671-64364-9

First Pocket Books printing January 1989

10 9 8 7 6 5 4 3 2 1

Printed in the U.S.A.

RED CENT

One

Every once in a while I get to feeling moody, just like everybody else. I start brooding about my time of life, what I've accomplished with it so far and what I can squeeze into the years left to me. A sense of my mortality descends on me like a blanket, blocking out the sun and making me melancholy.

I think about the Christmas trees I haven't decorated and the traditions I haven't carried on and the picnics I haven't organized as the head of a family. I think about having no one to carry on my name. There'll be plenty of Hatches, I suppose, but I don't know if there'll be any Jake Hatches, Jacob being an old-fashioned name that's fallen out of favor.

You come to a certain age and you start thinking about your roots.

You can hardly help it.

You start regretting that you hadn't listened harder when Aunt Jen or Uncle Frank told the familiar stories about how it was and where we all came from. Not even talked, just listened. But first there was radio and then television and the old ones in families got listened to less and less. It was all old news and nobody gave much of a damn.

I've got to go see my sister one of these days and ask her can I have duplicates made of all the family pictures. Me holding on to a toy wheelbarrow the year I broke my leg when I was six and hobbling around in a cast. The summer we all went to the seashore all the way over to Atlantic City. Ma and Pa's wedding picture. The picture of my old man squinting in the sun when he was small, with my grandmother standing behind him. And the picture of her when she was an infant sitting on *her* mother's knee.

My great-grandmother.

I don't boast about it, but I'm proud of the fact that there is more than a drop of Mohawk in my veins from my great-grandmother on my mother's side. She was called Moon of Spring. She trekked, the stories tell, into the wilderness of Canada with her husband, Adam Hatch, hunting and trapping.

They were wintering on the shores of Lake Winnipeg when my grandfather, the first Jake Hatch, was born. It was a hard birth and it looked like mother and child would die. But Adam journeyed with them down the Red River of the North to Fargo, North Dakota, where they settled for a while until both were well recovered. They became storekeepers in Pierre, South Dakota, then a small town on the banks of the Missouri.

When my grandfather was grown, he adventured throughout Nevada, Utah, Wyoming, and the Dakotas until he met my grandmother, who convinced him that Chadron, Nebraska, her hometown, was the place to take up the blacksmith's trade and raise a family.

When my own father was old enough to decide for

himself, he turned his back on the forge, although he'd been trained in its use since the age of nine, and became first a brakeman and then an engineer on the Burlington Northern. After he married, my mother and father settled just outside Ottumwa, Iowa. That's where I was born and raised. That's where I learned of my Mohawk blood. I already knew railroading was in my veins.

They're gone now, my mother and father.

I have two sisters and a brother. They live in other parts of the country. None of them wanted to work for the railroad like I did.

I worked a dozen different jobs on and around the trains until I sort of fell into what I've come to love best. I'm one of that dying breed—at least that's the way romantic writers describe us—the railroad detective.

I rent the second floor of a three flat in Omaha from Mrs. Dunleavy, who seems to appreciate my solitary habits and takes care of my cat when I'm away, which is often. She's just that much older than me that she feels free to share a stew now and then without being afraid that I'll think she's setting her cap.

I ride the route in the ordinary way about twice a week, which is to say I pretend to be a passenger and keep my eye out for ticket thieves, pickpockets, unauthorized vendors, and the like. It gives me an opportunity to stop off here and there and visit with some ladies of my acquaintance and other friends.

The rest of the time—about two full days—I catch up on paper work back in the office while my boss, Silas Spinks, nods off at his desk beside the window where the afternoon sun pours in and warms his back. But it was well past the hour of any sun, Spinks asleep and me tapping away on the typewriter, putting in overtime without pay, because neither of us had any special place to go or anybody waiting dinner for us at home, when the telephone on his desk jarred him awake.

He picked up, looking none too pleased, and grunted into the mouthpiece, mumbling what passed for a greeting, then uh-huhing and hoo-hooing for a couple of minutes.

"Oh, yeah, he did the right thing," he said, finally speaking English, "but you'd better ask the front office if they want the train delayed until one of us gets there. Seems to me the right thing to do would be to back the California Zephyr into Ottumwa and detach the dining car, get the Ottumwa police to seal it off and ask them, as a courtesy, not to be too fast jumping on the investigation until"—his eyes landed on me—"Hatch arrives."

He went back to grunting gibberish and then hung up.

"A passenger was having his dinner in the dining car about twenty minutes ago," he informed me. "Just outside Ottumwa going west. Some men in two pick-ups traveling parallel through the tulles along the right-of-way started firing off some rifles. One of the bullets came through the window and struck the passenger in the head."

"Dead?"

"As a doornail."

"I never heard of such a thing."

"Sure you have," Spinks said, casual as you please. "We ain't got but a few Indian reservations and settlements, but down along the southern Amtrak route, where there's plenty, Indians take random shots at the train all the time."

"Out to kill the Iron Horse?" I said.

"Something like that. So why don't you drive on over to Ottumwa in a company car and see what you can do?"

"What makes you think these men were Indians? Anybody get that close a look?"

"Well, I didn't say I thought they was Indians. I just said it happens down along the southern route that reservation Indians take potshots at the trains."

"They catch them?"

"The dispatcher didn't say."

"Well, if they caught them, that's that, and if they haven't, I don't know what I can do about it."

"We got to show the flag."

"Will this trip count as overtime?"

"How about we count it on your vacation?"

"The company already owes me eight or nine months accumulated."

"So, you ever decide to get married, look at the honeymoon you'll have."

Two

I LEFT OMAHA without any supper about eight-fifteen, the front office having taken the advice and deciding to detach the dining car from the train, not in Ottumwa, about twenty miles back along the line from where the accident occurred, but up the line in the direction of the run about sixty-three miles, at Osceola, which serves Des Moines.

They would arrive around ten-ten, forty minutes late. I'd get there about nine-fifteen by road, which meant I had a whole hour to spend along the way. There was no reason I could think of why I shouldn't stop in on Rose Palou, a widowed lady of my acquaintance who lives in a neat little cottage she owns in Van Meter.

Rose is a calm woman of generous disposition and outspoken honesty. The only thing a person might hold against her is her fondness for cats. There are always a half dozen or more draping themselves across the furniture, curling around your ankles, and leaving cat hairs on your dark suit. You can have a relationship with one cat. When they come in bunches they're nothing but a burden.

She never seems to mind it when I appear without warning, being of the mind that life is one long series of chance encounters anyway so why bother getting annoyed when something happens because it happens.

She met me at the door, having been alerted that someone was walking up the path by one of her sentry cats, and gave me a hug, which is something I tend to miss a lot, living alone the way I do.

"That," I said, "is just what the doctor ordered."

"Have you been ailing because deprived?" she said, letting me go and leading me into the parlor.

"It ain't the quantity of the embraces but the quality of them that counts," I said.

"My God, Jake, if I were a bird I'd've just fallen out of the tree and bonked my head. Are you here for a quickie?"

I couldn't believe my ears. What had Rose been getting up to, learning such language?

"I didn't quite catch your last remark, Rose."

"I asked did you stop by for a quick tumble in the feathers."

"For Lord's sake, where are you picking up words like that?"

"Don't you watch the television? Don't you go to the movies?"

"Well, I do sometimes, but that's that and—"

"What's what? I was asking if that was your idea, because the answer is no."

"Not that I came visiting for any such thing, Rose, but why did you say what you just said?"

"Because you're a careless, wandering vagabond, Jake, and that could lead to troublesome, even deadly, complications nowadays."

"Well, I can see precautions are called for in certain segments of the society to guard against fatal ailments, but I doubt if the crowd we run around with has much to fear."

"I don't run around in a crowd, Jake. It's you that has a crowd."

"I don't get your meaning."

"Well, you do, Jake. I've learned that when you say I don't get your meaning that's just when you got the meaning exactly."

"Where does that leave us, Rose?"

"It leaves us good friends, hugs and apple pie. Any more than that calls for a commitment you've not yet given."

"You know I'm not a marrying man, Rose."

"Fine. Now how would you like your pie, with or without whipped cream?"

"What do you think I should have?"

"Without. Then you can have a bowl of the fresh vegetable soup I've got simmering on the stove and some of my oatmeal bread."

Rose's vegetable soup is a poem and her oatmeal bread an essay on good eating. Sitting there at the kitchen table having such a meal made me think about the things we give each other, men and women. Love and comfort and support and kindness and sex and good things to eat and drink. I sometimes wonder, past a certain age, which is the greatest proof of affection.

"What brings you this way this time of night?" she asked, as she watched me eat.

"Trouble on the Zephyr. Some youngsters apparently hoo-rahed the train and took a couple of shots at it. A bullet killed a man sitting in the dining car having his dinner."

"I never heard of such a thing."

"I said the same thing, but Silas Spinks reminded

me that it happens now and then along the southern route."

"What's to be done about it?"

"I don't know. It's like the cages they have to put on the walkways over highways and freeways in the city to keep people from tossing bricks and stones through the windshields of the speeding cars. Can't build concrete walls the length of the railroad on both sides to protect them. Sometimes I think it's all got out of hand."

Rose shivered and looked away, past the frilly curtains at the window, out into the darkness of her garden where the oak leaves chattered in the wind.

"What is it?" I asked. "I didn't mean to distress you."

"Whenever I hear something like that or hear about it on the news, it makes me feel so unprotected. Even in a small town like this, where there's so little crime and violence, you think about how it only takes one creature passing through to take your life or hurt you so your life's changed forever after."

Every once in a while, when a woman of my acquaintance expresses such fears, it reminds me all over again how hard it must be for a woman to have to live her life with such anxieties as men only experience in small portion and then usually only when they're very young or very old.

"Well, I've got my tiger cats," she said, laughing and shaking her head until her curly hair bounced.

I finished my pie and a second cup of coffee.

"That's twice tonight you saved my life," I said. "Now I got to go and poke my nose into things I'd rather not poke it into."

"I doubt that," she said, walking me to the door, where she hugged me again and kissed me on the mouth. Still holding me, she said, "You ought to think about getting married, Jake, the state of the world and your health and all else considered." She placed her hand on my cheek. "Stop back if it's not past midnight, or in the morning if you stay over."

I went out, got in the company car, and drove off. *That's the first time she'd ever approached the subject of marriage head on. It made me nervous, not because she'd expressed her needs and desires but because I feared she might be expressing mine.*

I thought about it during the short drive into the train yards where the dining car waited and decided to talk it over with my cat when I got back home.

Three

THE YARD WAS DARK except for the carousels on two police cars and an ambulance splashing red light around.

Lights also shone out of the dining car, which had been separated from the train and shunted off to a spur. It looked like the funeral car of some great man waiting to be pulled a long way through the states while people stood along the right-of-way, waving flags and weeping.

I had no idea if the dead man inside was a great man or just a commonplace one like myself, riding the train home from some pleasure or business trip to Chicago, with maybe a wife and some kiddies waiting for him.

I parked alongside a sheriff's car and set the brake. It was cold enough to wear a topcoat but not cold enough to button it up. Flu weather.

There were places I'd've rather been.

A young uniformed officer got out of the car and

stepped over to me the way they do, moving at a speed that I call aggressive though not threatening.

I held up a hand, palm out, as I went for the wallet in my hip pocket.

"Don't get nervous, son. I'm a railroad detective."

He got loose, but not all at once. It was only after he saw my badge and I.D. that he took his hand off the butt of his gun.

"I shouldn't be so jumpy," he said.

"I'm jumpy and I ain't even seen the corpse yet. He still inside?"

"Sergeant Atterbury told the people from the morgue to wait until somebody from your office had a look."

"Well, I don't know what good me having a look is going to do. But I suppose it's better to look wise than foolish, so I might as well go in there, purse my lips, and cluck my tongue a little bit. Atterbury the man on the scene?"

"Well, it happened in county, so I guess he's the man."

"Didn't happen in this county. Happened in Monroe."

"Oh."

"I see a car from the Osceola Police Department is here. What's their particular interest?" I said.

"To see nobody steals the body, I suppose."

"That's good," I said. "You're making jokes. This your first homicide?"

"Oh, no, I've seen others, but not when what's in a person's head is splashed all over the walls."

"Not a pretty sight," I agreed.

The door to the dining car opened at the end nearest where we stood.

"I guess I better go do it," I said.

"I guess," he said and made a face.

I climbed the steps and showed my wallet to the sheriff sergeant standing there.

"How's Silas Spinks?" he asked.

"Mean as ever."

"You ready?"

"Ready as I'll ever be."

He moved back a step, flattening himself against the open door and letting me go in past him.

You'd never believe how much blood and brain matter is contained in a human head until you see it splattered all over a fairly confined space. The walls and the windows opposite the place where he'd been sitting looked like that artist, Jackson Pollack, had lost all his colors except red and gray. One window, though, had been blown out altogether.

The dead man was lying on his side on the floor as though he'd just tipped over and fallen there all curled up in a sitting position. The top of his head was gone and I knew the right side of his face was gone, too. He was wearing a dark blue pinstripe, black socks with maroon clocks, and black slip-ons. The cuff of his shirt showing at the wrist of one outflung arm was blue. He was lying on his tie.

A man I supposed was the medical examiner was leaning a hip on a table and staring at me, waiting to see if I'd lose my dinner.

I smiled at him and said, "Doctor?"

"Boulanger."

"My name's Jake Hatch. I'm a detective for the Burlington Northern working out of Omaha."

"We've been waiting for you."

"I thank you for it, but you didn't have to. I could've come to you."

He shrugged and said, "Well," accepting my remark as thanks, "I thought I'd save you the trip to Des Moines."

"I don't have to ask what killed him. I can see. What was the calibre of the bullet?"

"Don't know. A shot like that right here"—he tapped the middle of his forehead—"can pop the skull like a melon."

"I can see that. I was thinking somebody might've found the slug."

"Busted out the window on the other side."

I looked where he was pointing, though I'd already noticed it, and then I looked at Atterbury.

"First light in the morning I'll have men out there combing the right-of-way," he said.

"Needle in a haystack. Good luck."

"We'll do what we can do."

I glanced over at another table where a small pile of things a man would carry in his pockets were piled. A money clip, some coins, ring of keys, handkerchief, silver pocketknife, comb, billfold, thin calculator, and a purple plush ring box.

"Can I look?"

"Go ahead, help yourself."

I touched the money clip.

"Two hundred twenty-six dollars," Atterbury said. "Man's name is Harold Chaney."

"Oh?"

"Ring a bell?"

"Don't I see the name around?"

"If you ride the trains, and I guess you ride them plenty, you probably noticed the signs on factories along the line this side of Denver."

"Chaney Enterprises. Sure. Big business. Where was he coming from?"

"Chicago."

"Wonder why a man that rich don't fly."

"Afraid of planes, maybe."

Somebody way back in the far corner of the car cleared his throat. Sam Franklin, a dining car attendant I'd known for years, was sitting in the shadows in his red jacket.

"Hello, Mr. Franklin," I said. "What're you doing here?"

"They left me with the car."

"What the hell they do that for?"

"I haven't got the foggiest."

"The train had to go ahead," Atterbury said. "I guess they thought they should leave somebody to represent the company."

"Hear that, Sam? You're representing the company."

"I'd sooner be at home, Jake," Sam replied.

"Me too. So we're both here, how about you tell me what happened?"

He got up and came over to sit down in a chair closer to me. I took one facing.

"There's hot coffee on the sideboard," Sam said.

"I've had sufficient for the night. Be up till all hours as it is. So what time did it happen?"

"I'd say eight-thirty, eight-forty. Train was running an hour late but dinner service was as usual. I wanted to say that Mr. Chaney wasn't afraid of planes. He flew to Europe and Asia all the time. He just loved trains. Anytime business took him anywhere along the line he'd grab the chance to ride the train."

"You knew him pretty good?" Atterbury asked, as though accusing Sam of withholding information.

"As good as a waiter gets to know somebody he waits on as many times as I waited on Mr. Chaney."

"So he was a train buff?" I asked.

"I don't know was he an enthusiast. Just he said he loved riding the trains. Said he was afraid all this modern technology would wreck the railroads sooner or later."

"What happened during dinner?"

"Somebody made a remark about a bunch of crazy

kids racing the train alongside the tracks. I took a look. There were maybe five or six of them in two pickups driving through the tulles."

"Could you see faces?"

Sam shook his head and said no.

"Then what?"

"I went on about my business. I was back in the galley when I heard the pops."

"Rifle shots?"

"I guess that's what they were. Somebody even said, 'My God, those crazy people are shooting at us,' and somebody else said, 'They must be drunk,' and somebody else asked, 'Can they hit us?' and then—"

I reached out and patted his hand. "Take it easy. Take your time."

"It's getting harder to talk about it."

"Maybe you got a little shock setting in."

"I'll give him some tranquilizers to take home with him," Boulanger said. "He might have some nightmares."

"I'm not used to such things, Jake," Sam said.

"Neither am I. Whenever you're ready, Sam."

"It was right after whoever it was asked could they hit us when Mr. Chaney's head blew up and he fell on the floor."

"Okay, okay. Is it all right with everybody if Sam goes home?"

"I live back in Chicago," Sam said, with a rueful twist to his mouth.

"You already call your wife?"

He nodded.

"Well, call her again and tell her we're putting you up at a hotel here in Osceola. You can take the eastbound tomorrow. What time?"

"Nine o'clock in the morning."

"So, that's good. You'll get a night's sleep. I'll

arrange with the front office for you to have three days off."

"Thank you, Mr. Hatch," he said, getting to his feet.

"You're welcome, Mr. Franklin," I said, getting to mine.

He looked down at the man he'd served so many times.

"The Lord only knows," he said.

"Amen," Atterbury and I said together.

"Can I have a look at that ring box?" I asked.

Atterbury handed it to me and I opened it up. There was an emerald ring in it, must've been four or five carats.

The inside of the band was engraved with two little hearts on either side of the initials "PIP."

"I wonder if somebody was having a birthday," I said.

Four

FOR A MAN WHO works for the railroad I drive a car a lot. For a man who loves the railroad I'm *forced* to drive a car a lot. Maybe that's why medium-haul, city-to-city trains are dying, because we like to have our automobiles parked outside the door so we can come and go at a minute's notice. I have to admit, being tied to a schedule can make some jobs difficult.

Like the next morning after I woke up in the hotel closest to the depot. If I took the nine o'clock into Chicago, where Chaney'd lived, I wouldn't be along the right-of-way when the slug was found. If it was found.

Having the company car right there, I decided I could drive back along to Ottumwa and see how the search was going, maybe even lend a hand, even if it made me feel like a traitor.

The search for the bullet had been going on since sunup, but by the time I found the search party along the right-of-way it still hadn't been found. Atterbury was in charge of half a dozen deputies and about the same number of uniforms from Osceola. There were even a few civilians and some boy scouts combing through the trash and weeds along the right-of-way with metal detectors, like they were looking for nickels on the beach.

He shook my hand and we stood there watching the line of men and boys moving along the track close enough so they could touch finger ends if they raised their arms. Every once in a while one of them would squat down and finger something he'd found and then stand up again to keep shuffling along, looking.

"This is the eighth pass," Atterbury said. "I'm about ready to give it up."

"Hard as hell to know when to quit a search like this."

"Well, at least we got some idea of what kind of slug we're looking for. Boulanger took the body to Des Moines last night and, late as it was, ran some tests. Found particles of cupronickel around the entry wound."

"Is there something I should know from that?"

"Boulanger says the English are the only commercial loaders still using cupronickel jacketing."

"Well, that's something, I suppose," I said. "One of these days we could come across somebody with a pocketful of foreign cartridges."

"I won't hold my breath," Atterbury said.

"I was going to give you a hand," I said, "but it doesn't look to me like one more pair of eyes'd do much good."

"Probably no amount of eyes would. Bullet hit the window, then a skull, then a window again. Probably busted up into little bits the size of BBs, the way it blew that window out."

We stood there chewing that one over until Atterbury said, "They caught the kids that done it."

"Kids?"

"Six of them. Ages seventeen through twenty-two or -three. Indians."

"From the Mesquakie Settlement?" I asked.

"They say not. Claim to be just visiting relatives."

"From where?"

"From the Santee Sioux Reservation up along the Dakota border."

"Mesquakie is Sac and Fox. No relative to the Sioux."

"Well, it could still mean the Bureau of Indian Affairs could get into the act." Atterbury didn't look any too pleased about that. It was always a mess when too many agencies of one sort or another started stirring the pot.

"The murder, if that's what it is, didn't occur on the reservation. Maybe it's like a soldier committing a crime off the post."

"They could still be tried in the civil courts."

"Except reservation Indians are under special treaty with the United States government. They're treated like sovereign nations. They've got their own police and their own powers to prosecute and punish. On top of which you say some are underage? Complications."

"Maybe I'm the one who's got the easy part, trying to find some bits of lead along a five-mile right-of-way full of trash."

"I'm not doing any good here," I said.

"Where you off to?"

"Thought I'd drive over to the morgue and have another talk with Boulanger. Then I think I'll look in on those boys in jail. You happen to know where they're keeping them?"

"Indianola, but there's talk of moving them."

"What the hell? Not a bit of this took place in Warren County."

"It's where they were arrested on Route Sixty-five.

But, you're right, the shooting took place in Monroe County. If I was you, I'd call first. Otherwise, you're going to be driving all over Iowa."

"I'll do that," I said, and started walking.

I'd walked off about three strides when Atterbury called out to me. I turned around to hear what he had to say.

"What did you mean by what you just said?" Atterbury asked.

"You mean about having another talk with Boulanger?"

"No, about it maybe being murder."

"Well, I don't know yet, but I'm wondering a little about where a bunch of young fellas like them Indians would get their hands on a rifle capable of throwing a slug that'd do that much damage and then disappear out the window."

Five

I'm not going to describe the morgue in Des Moines. Morgues are morgues, only some are less crowded and cleaner than others.

Boulanger's operation was run tight and clean. You could tell the minute you stepped in the door that nobody was going to end up missing because of carelessness. Nobody's heart or liver was going to be misfiled or tossed in the trash by mistake.

To get to the office Boulanger had chosen for himself you had to walk through the autopsy room. There were no corpses waiting for attention and that was all right with me.

He was sitting behind a pane of glass so he could see what was going on in the laboratory, and he looked up when he heard my heels tapping the tiles.

He half stood up to shake my hand when I walked through the door, then sat right back down again and asked me to do the same.

"Atterbury told me you found cupronickel traces in the entry wound," I said.

"Yes, I did. I don't know if that's any help."

"It would be if we could find it or if we find the rifle loaded with cupronickel-jacketed bullets. You happen to know what kind of cartridges those Indian boys were using?"

"Nothing's been brought to our ballistics yet. Anyway, do you think you can make the case on the evidence of a bullet?"

"It's not my case to make," I said. "It's not even in my hands. I'm just curious about a thing or two."

"Like what?"

"Oh, like is this an accident caused by a bunch of wild kids out hoo-rahing a train or is it a case of murder."

"Murder? For God's sake, Hatch, isn't that reaching for it? We've got a bunch of wild-assed kids with too many beers in them raising a little hell that got way out of hand."

"In my experience," I said, "murder's almost always too much for people to believe. How often do you hear it on the news how some man or boy, after killing off six or seven people, family and friends, is described by everyone who ever knew him as a very mild-mannered, quiet person who liked to read books and take long walks through the woods with his dog? People just can't believe he'd do murder without apparent reason."

"But there's a reason found sooner or later, no matter how crazy it may seem."

"Well, it's early times and I'm not ready to say this is anything but death by misadventure," I said. "How old a man was Mr. Chaney?"

"According to his driver's license he was fifty-eight."

"In good health?"

"Better than most men his age."

The intercom on the desk sounded. Boulanger hit the toggle.

"Mrs. Chaney is here," a woman's voice said.

"I'll be right there," Boulanger replied.

"You going to ask her to make an identification?"

"It's a requirement of the law."

"How you going to handle it? The man's not recognizable."

"I've got his clothes and his personal belongings. I've got a description of marks and scars and a dental chart of crowns and fillings. He had a practically new three-tooth bridge. I'll make it as easy as I can."

"You mind if I come along?"

"I don't see why not."

We stood up.

"I don't think introductions are called for at a time like this," I said.

He nodded and I followed him out through the laboratory to the reception room.

I held back and let Boulanger get up ahead of me when he walked up to the woman, who was standing there with her arms holding herself. She was a good-looking woman who looked to be on the low side of forty. But you can't really tell these days. I have a friend, Lula Rippard, looks thirty and she's sixty.

But, forty or whatever, Mrs. Chaney was a thoroughbred. She had the fine bones and the long legs, the deep chest and the glossy mane. If she knew what I was thinking she might've been insulted being described like she was a mare, but I doubt it. I think it would be the kind of appreciation she could understand and enjoy.

She was wearing a greenish-brown tweed suit and brown walking shoes, with a tan topcoat draped over her shoulders. No hat. No furs. No jewelry, that I could see, except for a pin on her lapel and a wedding ring on her finger.

She was giving all her attention to Boulanger as he shook her hand, then held it as he explained the procedure. Only once did she give me a glance. I could see she was wondering who I might be, but wouldn't ask.

There was a man in, I'd say, his late thirties, who'd been sitting down when we walked in, but who'd stood up and was standing beside Mrs. Chaney now with his arm around her shoulders as though ready to steady her if she needed it. She acted like she didn't know he was there.

She nodded her head once and said, "I understand," and then disengaged herself from the man's arm. "You wait here, Lewis."

"Are you sure, Florence?"

She patted his hand as though he was the one needing comfort and said she was sure.

Boulanger held the door to the viewing room for her but let me follow him in by a step or two.

There was a table in the middle of the small room, which had one wall of glass that looked out onto the laboratory just like Boulanger's office did.

The attendant at the desk, who'd left when we appeared, had gone to get Harold Chaney's things. He was standing on the other side of the glass now, waiting in case anything more was wanted.

There was an official folder and Chaney's belongings set out neatly in a row. Boulanger picked up the file and opened it.

"Is this what I'm to identify?" Mrs. Chaney asked. Her voice was sweet and husky, as though she'd been crying a good deal and had worn it out.

"If you can first identify these personal effects and then corroborate medical evidence I'll enumerate, I think we can spare you having to view the body."

She looked at him with the levelest gaze I'd seen in a long time, thinking over what he'd said.

"What sort of medical evidence?"

"Did your husband have an appendectomy scar?"

"Yes."

"Did he have a small scar on his right knee?"

"Yes."

"Did he have a mole just above his right hipbone?"

Boulanger put his thumb on his own hip to indicate the place.

"Yes," Mrs. Chaney said.

"Any other identifying marks or scars?"

"A birthmark about the size of a strawberry just above his left eyebrow at the hairline."

"I'm afraid I can't corroborate that," Boulanger said, looking at her as steadily as she was looking at him.

Her face spasmed for a moment like a baby about to yell, then became passive again. "Oh," she said very softly.

She'd read it all and said she'd understood in that single word.

"Your husband had some dental work."

She shook her head and made a little noise like laughter or denial.

"I'm not sure I could tell you which tooth was capped and which was filled."

"He had a three-tooth bridge put in recently."

"If he did, I wouldn't know about it. Harold was very private about such things. Does it seem strange I wouldn't know about something like that?"

"Not strange at all," Boulanger said.

"Was that enough?" she asked.

"I think I can certify that you've made a proper identification."

"There must be a million men who've had their

appendix out and carry a playground scar on their knee."

"And the mole. Three out of three."

"Even so. Perhaps we should be sure. I'd like to be sure."

"The bullet did a great deal of damage to your husband's head and face."

"I won't look at that. I'll just look at his hands. I'll know if it's him by looking at his hands. He had beautiful, expressive hands."

Boulanger looked at the attendant and nodded his head. The attendant went into the locker and came out a few minutes later with a sheet-draped body on a gurney.

"No, no," Mrs. Chaney said. "Not from a distance. I won't be able to tell anything for sure from a distance."

I stayed where I was, watching through the window, as Boulanger took Mrs. Chaney into the laboratory and up to her husband's body.

He hesitated a moment, then undraped Chaney's hand and arm.

She lifted her husband's hand in one of her own, then covered it with her other hand. She stared at it softly as though she finally believed he was truly dead.

Then she carefully replaced his hand along his side, turned, and walked out as though it was time to get on with whatever needed doing.

Six

I TOOK THE CHANCE and stopped at the jailhouse in Indianola without calling first. I knew the chief of police, Ray Levi, a home-grown cop who had a year to go for his retirement.

He was in his office, which was something of a surprise, since he's the kind of working chief who leaves the paperwork to his assistant and likes to go off in a car, seeing how his town's doing.

"Hello, Jake," he said, getting up to greet me and shake my hand. "Don't tell me, you're here to see the war party shot up your train last evening."

"You still got them here?"

"We've only got a two-cell jail for drunks and vagrants, Jake, but I guess we can hold them long enough for them to make up their minds about who's taking jurisdiction."

"Who's them?"

"State attorney general's office, I suppose. Or maybe the governor's office itself."

"Is there interest on that level already?"

"Sure there's interest. I got a call from the district attorney to stay close to my charges until they're transferred because, if I lost them, I could begin worrying about getting fired before my retirement. Without a pension."

"I doubt that."

"I doubt it too. They were just trying to make a point and they made their point. Chaney's a very important man with very important connections."

"But we're probably talking about accidental manslaughter here, Ray."

"Are we?"

"Aren't we?"

"Well, I'll tell you, Jake, if I was a betting man I wouldn't bet you a hundred dollars to a red cent that one or all of those Indian boys in there ain't going to pay a big price for their little hour of fun and games."

Seven

The young Indians were jailed three men to a cell, meaning two had the over-under bunks and one slept on a mattress on the floor in each of them.

I had the turnkey let me inside the first cage and told him I'd give him a call.

"Just yell for Monk," the turnkey said.

I leaned my back against the bars, told the three boys who I was, and asked them to give me their names.

"Do me a favor and don't give me your Indian names. I won't understand them and won't remember them. Don't give me their English equivalents. I'm not going to ask Black Sky in the Morning or Buffalo Walks Through the Snow any questions. I want to talk to Jim or Joe or Ben. Whatever you're called in public."

"White man's names."

"That's right."

"So you don't want to take the time to know us, is that it?" the best-looking of the youngsters said.

When I say best-looking I don't mean best-looking by white standards, by moving-picture standards. I mean best-looking by Indian standards.

His complexion was dusky like there was a fire burning just under tanned hide. He had the Mongolian upper eyelid which meant he had practically none at all. The color of his eyes was such a dark brown it was almost black and the whites were yellowish. He had sharp, high cheekbones and a nose like a hawk's bill. I could just bet the young women on the reservation were nuts about him.

"Oh, I'm going to take the time to know you. You can bet your wikiup on that. I mean no disrespect when I ask you to make it easy on me. I won't insult you but I won't pussyfoot around for fear of hurting your feelings because I don't know how sensitive you might be about this or that. So I told you my name was Jake. Give me something to call you."

The kid sitting on the top bunk in jeans and plaid workshirt, with his bare feet dangling, said, "They call me Rider. That's what they call me, so that's what you better call me."

"Okay, Rider, it's short and sweet. You?"

The one laying on the lower bunk with his hands propping his head up said, "Willy."

"That's good. Had a friend named Willy when I was a boy. Hell of a nice guy . . ."

"Glad to hear it."

". . . except he was a terrible liar. I hope you ain't a terrible liar, Willy. Hope none of you are terrible liars because, believe it or not, I'm here to help you and I can't very well help you if I don't know the truth."

The Indian who looked most like an Indian, the one sitting scrunched up in blue work pants and shirt and cowboy boots, said, "Maybe we should cut our thumbs and mix our blood. Then you could be sure."

The other two laughed.

"Blood brothers don't lie to each other."

"If that's what it'll take, that's what we'll do. But for right now, how about you just give me a name."

"Abe."

"Do you want to tell me, Abe, what happened Saturday night?"

"We left the reservation around four in the afternoon. Drove down to Wahoo for some barbecue and a couple of beers."

"Why didn't you stay closer, like in Tama?"

"Tama's practically inside the reservation. We didn't feel like staying inside the reservation."

"Took Route Seventy-seven?"

"That's right."

"I make that about sixty-four miles."

"Give or take."

"Hour and a half?"

"Hour."

"So, you're in Wahoo."

"We go to the Texas Cattle Room. You know it?"

"I know every place to eat, thirty miles each side of the right-of-way."

He looked at my gut, which has been getting somewhat bigger with the onslaught of age, and touched his own belly, which was probably like a washboard underneath his shirt, and said, "So we order barbecue."

"Ribs?"

"Yeah, ribs. And some beef and chicken."

"Couple pitchers of beer?"

They stole glances at one another, acting like nothing but kids after all was said and done, and Rider smirked as though they'd put one over.

"More than a couple?" I asked.

"Yeah, more than a couple," Willy said.

"Got drunk?"

"Got feeling good," Abe said.

"How good?"

They tossed around the same silly, secret looks and smiles.

"Good enough to start telling stories?"

Abe nodded.

"Good enough to have a braggin' contest?"

"What do you know about bragging contests?"

"If you get the chance, ask some of your old men about Jake Hatch. Ask them who was the big liar around the campfires when we went out hunting."

"Hunting what?"

"Hunting poon," Rider said, with this little smirk.

He got his laugh.

"Funny thing, when I was your age, when your fathers were your age, we wouldn't make jokes about hunting. Maybe they were closer to the old ways."

"So you know about our ways?"

"I know enough to know what a bragging contest is. What did you come to brag most and best about? After you exhausted the lies about all the pretty ass you'd captured?"

"Family."

"Okay. I understand that. You bragged about what your clans did in the days when they owned the land."

"Nobody owns the land."

"I stand corrected. When the tribes fought for their ways."

"Fought to kill the goddamn white eyes who invaded our nations with whiskey, guns, and smallpox, shit in our streams, plowed up our burial grounds, and drove the trains like a spear through the heart of our country."

"So you decided to kill the goddamn Iron Horse," I said.

"That's right. That's right," they all said. Broke up at the memory of it. Willy almost rolling off his bunk with pleasure at the marvelous foolishness of their drunkenness. Rider throwing his legs over his head, then bringing his knees down to his stomach, ripping off a fart and not apologizing for it, because Indians don't think that such evidence of humanity is shameful or impolite. Abe just sat there with his forearms resting on his knees, his head lowered, shaking it from side to side until his blue-black hair fell loose around his cheeks.

"You decided to slay the Iron Horse just like your ancestors tried to do a hundred years ago?"

"Bring that sonofabitch to its knees like a brain-shot buffalo," Rider said, beside himself with joy.

"How'd you do it?"

They stopped laughing. It was like they were drunk for a minute and now they were sobered up.

"We got a couple of six-packs and piled into the pickups," Abe said. "We drove down Sixty-three and One Thirty-seven to H Thirty-five, ran alongside the tracks for a few miles, and when we heard the train coming, left the road altogether. Both trucks got oversized tires and four-wheel drives, so when we got off into the tulles it was no trouble driving through the loose stuff."

"How were the rifles spread out?"

"What do you mean?" Abe asked.

"I mean where the hell were they? How many in the racks? Any in a boot under the dash? How do you carry the goddamn things?"

"I keep a pair of twenty-twos in a rack behind the seat and I had a thirty-thirty in my lap," Willy said.

"What have you got, a goddamn arsenal?"

"Different guns for different game," Willy said.

"Were you driving your truck?"

"No, I let Abe drive and was sitting alongside."

"I was driving Charlie's four-wheel," Rider said. "I think he keeps a thirty-ought-six in a boot under the dash. Dan Pool had his twenty-two with him in his hand."

"So, was your thirty-ought-six under the dash or on your lap, Charlie?" I said, lifting my voice so it'd carry next door.

"Under the dash. I had a little-bitty twenty-two in my lap."

"All right now," I said, taking out a pad and a ballpoint pen. "I want you to get more specific about these rifles. You first, Charlie."

"It's a Winchester two-fifty lever action."

I wrote that down. "What kind of cartridges?"

"Twenty-two Hornets."

"You next, Dan Pool."

"My rifle's a two-twenty Swift. Remington ammunition."

"How about you, Rider?"

"I was driving the truck."

"I know that, but I've heard of a man steering with his knees and taking a shot at running game."

"I had my thirty-thirty on the seat beside me."

"Just for my information, what make and model?"

"Winchester seven four two. Remington thirty-thirties."

"Okay, back to you for a minute, Abe. Where was your weapon?"

"It was on the seat between me and Willy."

"What kind?"

"Over-and-under shotgun."

"We can forget that. So Rider, Charlie, and Dan Pool were in one truck," I said. "You, Willy, and who else in the one you were driving?"

"Calgary. He's right next door."

"You listening to all this, Calgary? The rest of you boys?" I said, raising my voice again.

"Yes, sir," came back an answer so polite it surprised me. Maybe I'd picked the wrong crew to talk to first.

"Well, that's good. No sense me going through this session twice. Any comments you want to make, just speak up."

Nobody answered, so I went on.

"What were you totin', Calgary?"

"Model ninety-four Winchester carbine loaded with Remingtons," he said from the next cell.

"Where were you ridin'?"

"In the truck bed in Willy's truck."

"Who was in the truck bed in the truck you were drivin', Rider?"

"Me, Dan Pool," a voice said from the next cell. "Who gives a damn where anybody was riding?"

"You just answer a few more questions, boys, and then you'll get to ask me a couple. So you saw the train coming down the track."

"We're kicking up dust right alongside."

"How far alongside?"

"A little better than a quarter of a mile maybe."

"Sometimes more like half," Willy said.

"It's what time by now?" I asked.

"Eight o'clock. Maybe eight-thirty."

"Dark."

"There was a moon, but dark enough."

"Could see into the train cars real clear, though," Willy said. "Some of the people saw us, saw our lights—"

"The moon would've lighted us up some. The dust cloud behind us was silvered up," Abe interrupted.

"That figures. So the passengers on the train saw a couple of pickups racing the train."

"People in the diner looked up from their plates and couldn't believe their eyes. One guy lifted his glass like he was offering me a drink," Willy said. "As if I could've got to it."

"Who took the first shot?" I asked all of a sudden.

They all turned into wooden Indians. The next they'd do is grunt and wrap their blankets around themselves. I knew there were three more stone-faced statues in the next cell.

"Let me guess. It sure wasn't one of you driving the trucks. I doubt if it was Willy or Charlie sitting on the passenger side. I think it must've been either Dan Pool or Calgary, one of the boys in the truck beds."

"It was me, Dan Pool."

"Well, I pumped one off about the same time," Calgary said.

"We were all pumping them off a couple of seconds after the first round, so what difference does it make?" Willy said.

"You fire your rifle, Rider?"

"Sure I did. I had Charlie hold the wheel steady and I plinked a couple."

"Hit anything?"

"How the hell should I know? I wasn't exactly trying to do any damage to a train at four hundred yards."

"Sure not? How about you, Abe? You get one of Willy's extra rifles out of the overhead rack?"

"Never had the chance."

"All right, fellas, that's about all for now, I guess."

"You said we could ask you a couple of questions," Calgary said. "When the hell's Jim Willows coming over to get us the hell out of here?"

"Jim Willows, the chief at Mesquakie?"

"That's what he calls himself."

"I imagine Jim Willows has got his hands full trying to figure out jurisdiction here, but he's right on top of it, you can bet." I put my face between the bars and yelled, "Hey, Monk! I promise to be good! You can let me out now!"

I gave the boys a grin, letting them know that I could be funny, too, when I had a mind.

Monk came through the door to the office jingling his keys. He unlocked the cell door and I stepped out.

"Hey, I got a couple of questions," Rider said from the next cell.

I stepped over and looked through the bars. A young Indian I supposed was Charlie was huddled up against the wall and would hardly look at me. Another tall fella was lying facedown on the bunk. I couldn't get a look at him except for his hair, which was long and black.

"You said you'd answer a few," the third one, standing up to the bars, said.

"Save them, will you?" I said. "I've got no answers. The reason I wanted to talk to you boys all together was so you could hear what was said and get together on a story. One for all and all for one. I want to play fair. I want to give you every chance to get an act together so you won't think anybody's taking advantage."

"Goddammit, Rider, let him get the hell out of here. Don't play into their fucking games," Dan Pool said, his voice muffled by the blanket covering the cot.

Eight

IT'S ABOUT A HUNDRED AND FORTY-FIVE railroad miles from Des Moines to Omaha. I don't know exactly how many by highway. Short enough, anyway, for me to get home before nightfall even with a stop in Creston, Iowa, along the way.

There's an unmarried lady of my acquaintance lives in Creston who knows as much about firearms and ammunition as anyone I know. Her family have been gun dealers for three generations and she almost married a man devoted to guns except they had a quarrel over who was the fastest on the draw pulling from a regular holster and not one of those fancy exhibition rigs. She beat him. That's not to say she shot him dead. They were firing competition lasers with the look and heft of .45 revolvers. She beat him five times in a row and I suppose he just couldn't live with that.

There's been times when Catalina has challenged me to this game of skill or that contest of agility and endurance. There's only one I've ever agreed to. She outlasted me. She outlasted me five times in a row, but then she's considerably younger than me and I know when losing ain't losing.

Her house is far enough out of town that she can keep horses and dogs and cats and goats and I don't know what all else. Every time I drive or walk up to her kitchen door these creatures set up a hell of a racket.

When I stepped out of my car around four o'clock in the afternoon, the biggest gander I ever saw came running around the corner of the tool shed. I was in no mood to get into a territorial dispute, so I jumped up on the hood.

He stood there, neck outstretched, hissing at me until Catalina came out laughing to beat the band and shook her apron at him.

"Well, aren't you the brave one?" she said, her fine blond hair breaking loose from the bun in the back of her head and whirling around her face.

I got down with a sheepish smile on my face. It always pleases Catalina when I act like she's caught me out in some foolishness or some weakness, though I hope she knows it's just a game so far as I'm concerned.

"What brings you calling?" she asked.

"The hope of heaven," I said.

"If your idea of heaven is what I think is your idea of heaven, you'd better just put it aside."

"I always thought your idea of heaven was the same as mine."

"God, you can be coy when you want to be. What I'm saying is I've lost my appetite for casual dalliance . . ."

"There's a nice old-fashioned word."

". . . and such pastimes. There'll be no more slap and tickle, Jake. It's time we both grew up . . ."

I didn't want to hear what I knew was coming next.

". . . and thought about a grown-up relationship."

"I never thought you were a marrying woman. That's what you always said."

"That's what I said and that's what I meant." She ran her brown hand across her hair, smoothing it back out of her eyes. "But there's silver threads among the gold now, Jake."

"In case you haven't noticed, I haven't been standing still."

"A little snow looks good on a man like you, Jake. It's different for a woman."

"I never thought of you as a woman," I said as I followed her through the mud room and into the kitchen.

She tossed a look at me over her shoulder.

"That didn't come out exactly the way I meant it," I said, practically stumbling over my apology, my thoughts being so confused what with two lady friends in a row giving me veiled ultimatums.

"I know you didn't, Jake. You've proven to me often enough that you don't have any doubts about my gender. Just like I don't have any doubts about yours. However, I've been thinking about it and I think it's time for me to stop being frivolous."

I sat down at the kitchen table. It was covered with new oilcloth with a pattern I remembered being on my mother's kitchen table when I was a boy. At least some things didn't change.

"I like the oilcloth," I said, running my hand back and forth over the slick surface.

"It's a pretty pattern, isn't it? The storekeeper says that's the last of it. The company that makes it went out of business six months ago."

It looked to me, so far as women were concerned, I was going out of business too.

"It might look like I stopped by for comfort or

recreation, Catalina," I said, "but the truth is I came to pick your brain."

"About what?" she asked, taking some homemade wheat-raisin bread from the keeper and cutting off several slices.

"Guns and ammunition."

While she toasted the bread and got out a tub of sweet butter, I filled her in about what had happened to Mr. Chaney and the conditions of the shooting so far as I knew them.

"You think to take down the make and model of the rifles and the kind of cartridges they used?"

I grinned with satisfaction. Catalina knows I hate firearms of any sort and know less about them than any self-respecting country boy should know. Even when I was a youngster, after being blooded, I couldn't see the excitement in going out and killing some small animal, like a rabbit or a squirrel, who'd never done me any harm. When she wants to chide me about my squeamishness, she points out that I don't hesitate a minute to wolf down the saddle of venison she's butchered out of a deer she's shot with her own hands.

We could argue about that for a lifetime and come to no conclusion. Those who love to hunt will talk about thinning herds and keeping down rodents, and those who hate the idea of killing helpless animals'll still eat meat and wear leather shoes.

She looked over my list and nodded her head.

"How long a shot?"

"Anywhere from three hundred to four hundred yards."

"No," she said.

"An accidental bull's-eye?"

"Anything's possible. But with the trucks bouncing, train moving at a different speed, catching up or falling behind, rifles firing at random, an accidental hit is very unlikely."

"Would it be less unlikely with a scope?"

"A deliberate shot with a scope from a moving vehicle? Ever try to keep a gull in the field of a pair of binoculars when you were standing on the deck of a boat? Making a shot with a scope from a pickup would be worse than firing from the hip if you wanted to hit something. Field of vision'd jiggle all over the place. I'm also saying no because from this list of rifles and the description of the ammunition they used the bullet wouldn't have acted the way you say it acted."

"The coroner found traces of cupronickel," I said.

"English slugs."

"So, tell me about what bullets and rifles were probably used."

I won't go telling you what she told me, because it would only confuse you as much as it confused me. I wasn't just flattering Catalina asking her to give me lessons about weight and muzzle velocity and trajectories and penetrating power. Since I didn't know much, I was hoping that if I listened to all she had to say, she'd finally say something that was useful to me. And she did.

"The way you describe the damage to the head and blowing the back window out the way you said it did, I think I can describe the bullet and how it performed. Now, just about any bullet hitting just right could explode a man's head, and there are several can do the job as you describe it—though few could do so at the distance—so this is an educated guess."

"I won't be taking it into a court of law."

"The bullet went clean through the glass, then hit the victim, spread out, and broke up, smashing his head and going on through. By the time it hit the window it was like a load of buckshot and blew it out.

So, first of all, the cartridge was an oversized twenty-two or something bigger. Probably a thirty-thirty or a thirty-ought-six—which the six in this case doesn't designate the load of powder but because it was the U.S. military cartridge modified to its present form in nineteen hundred and six."

"These footnotes are very interesting, Catalina," I said, "but I'm afraid they'll only get me all confused. Are you saying the bullet was high-powered?"

"Probably not. Too high-powered and a bullet hitting a living target could go right on through. Then you find yourself tracking a lion or a wild boar through the bush. The idea is to deliver a bullet that will penetrate, then spread out and deliver a killing wound. You're probably looking for what remains of a hunting round, maybe a hundred-and-fifty-grain soft-point fired from a rifle that has a muzzle velocity of three thousand foot-seconds. Probably a wildcat cartridge."

"How's that?"

"A wildcat's a cartridge that's no longer in production. Somebody fancies they need a cartridge a little different than any available for a certain job, so they rework and reload an existing case and fit their own specs."

"Who'd do that sort of thing?"

"Enthusiasts get on to it. What you'd call gun nuts. Some competition shooters. Some hunters."

"Can they get it done?"

"I suppose some gun shops would find a craftsman prepared to make tailor-made loads but, mostly, they do the reloads themselves."

"So a hundred-and-fifty-grain wildcat cartridge with a soft-point bullet finished with cupronickel fired from a thirty-ought-six rifle."

"With a scope."

"You just now said a scope would be a drawback

trying a shot from a moving vehicle at a moving target."

"Well, that's just it, Jake. Unless they stashed the rifle or threw it away altogether, nothing on your list could do the job the way you tell it. The shot couldn't have been made from a moving vehicle, not if it was deliberate. I'd be willing to bet the shot was made by a shooter laying prone, resting the barrel of the rifle on a tripod or a mound."

Nine

Catalina invited me to supper. I thanked her kindly and said I'd best be on my way.

"I hope you understand my feelings about the other," she said.

I allowed as how these were trying times and we all had to muddle along as best we could, not letting her off the hook altogether.

"It's not for spite you won't stay for supper?" she asked.

I put my arms around her and held her for a little, whispering into her hair the way ladies like you to do, saying, "If we were never to lie close together again, Catalina, I'd still always remember you as one of the treasures of my life."

That made her shiver a little, but she still let me walk out the door.

The sun was going down. It lay at my back so that I was chasing the shadow of the car along the highway.

By the time I got to the outskirts of Omaha, two and

a half hours later, it was dark and I was feeling hungry, a little sorry I hadn't taken Catalina up on her offer of a meal since now all I had to face was a frozen dinner.

I knocked on my landlady, Mrs. Dunleavy's, door and asked her did anything much happen while I'd been gone. She said since I'd only been gone overnight, she expected things were much as they were except that Barney had come home with a torn ear and I really should get him neutered, if not to keep down the cat population of the neighborhood, at least to keep him from fighting and maybe getting himself killed.

She didn't invite me to stay for supper.

I went up the back way. Barney was on the porch off the kitchen and gave me a look that said if I'd stay home more often maybe he wouldn't go out seeking companions and getting himself tangled up in the wrong crowd.

I let him in through the door and hit the light. I got his dish and put half a can of cat food in it.

"Where you been eating while I've been gone?"

He told me.

"Down at the Chinese restaurant, hey? Well, there's your trouble."

He asked what trouble.

"That monosodium glutamate, MSG, they put in their food. Throws your metabolism all out of whack. Makes you nervous and careless. That's why you got your ass kicked."

He told me what I could do with my preaching.

Instead of a frozen dinner, I opened a can of soup and toasted a three-day-old roll I found in the bread box. I ate it feeling sorry for myself, which some people would say would show how foolish I am since I've had more than one chance to marry and settle down. More than one chance to just live with someone, for that matter. I choose to live alone but I don't see that means I gave away the right to feel lonesome every now and then.

The next morning I was up and at the office even before Spinks walked through the door.

"You look into that little matter up the line?" he asked.

"It was no little matter. A passenger had his head blown off."

Spinks looked at me as though testing the truth of that.

"I mean that like I said it," I added.

"Clean off?"

"Well, it wasn't clean."

"Get the men who done it?"

"They were Indians, just like you thought."

"I never thought they were Indians, but it figures."

"What figures?"

"It figures Indians or Mexicans would do something like that."

"Not drunken redneck white men, though?"

"Was they white men?"

"No, they were Indians."

"So what the hell are we disputing?"

"How the hell do I know?"

"Something biting your ass?"

What was biting my ass was that a man I'd worked with for years, a good and loyal friend, had just let it drop that he had a casual bias against Indians and Mexicans and didn't even know it. If I took exception, he wouldn't know what the hell I was talking about. There're more people like that than I'd like to count.

"No. Nothing like that."

"Then like what?"

"It seems everybody's ready to accept this as an unfortunate accident. Maybe charge these young Indians with involuntary manslaughter. Give them all a few years apiece to think about discharging firearms in such a careless way."

"That sounds fair to me. There's a lot of talk lately of cracking down on drunk drivers. What they did was just as irresponsible."

"I don't deny that. If they fired the shot that killed the man."

"What makes you think they didn't?"

"My bones."

"I don't want to hear about your bones."

"I read, not long ago, that great detectives work on instinct more than they do on reason."

"Be that as it may, what we got here is something that's really none of our business. I can't let you waste time on it. The front office'd raise hell, great detective or no great detective. You want to nose around something like this, you'll have to do it on your own time."

"You mean I'd have to use up vacation if I was to take a day or two just to poke around here and there?"

"How about this?" Spinks said. "I'll put you down for sixteen hours overtime added to your accumulated vacation. I'll let you have the use of a company car."

"How about the gasoline?"

"As long as you don't drive to California, you can put it on the company credit card."

"Expenses?"

"Don't test my good nature. You find yourself away from home at mealtime or at night, you'll just have to visit one of your widows, divorcees, or maiden ladies. That should be no hardship. You decided what you want to do?"

"Well, for one thing, I want to talk to the dead man's wife again."

"Where's she at?"

"I saw her in Des Moines at the morgue but I'm sure she'll be in Chicago by tonight."

"Okay. Meanwhile, type me up a report."

"What do you want me to put under cause of death?"

"Why, misadventure, what the hell else?"

Ten

It started to rain around three in the morning. Barney came rushing in off the back porch through the window in the kitchen I keep cracked a couple of inches, knocking over a jam jar full of pennies on the sill in his hurry to get in out of the wet.

Barney likes to gallivant but he don't like to stay out in bad weather.

He came in and sat on my feet, glowering at me like I was the one who spoiled his fun.

"Wise up," I said. "It's got nothing to do with the wind and the wet, Barney, it's old age creeping up on both of us. If either of us had any brains we'd get ourselves a wife and settle down in front of the fire and stop running around the countryside."

He reminded me we didn't have a fire to sit in front of.

"We could get one," I said, and rolled over for another forty winks.

When I got up at my usual hour of five, it was raining in earnest, beating against the windows in bursts and gusts like the rain itself wanted to get in where it was warm.

After I dressed and fed Barney and myself, I decided, convenience or no convenience, I'd take the train into Chicago and use taxicabs when I got there. Driving through the rain can be an unnerving occupation, giving you no chance to mull things over as you tootle along, but slashing through a storm on a train is almost like an adventure. The speed of the train makes the rain do tricks as it gets blown away in sheets by the speed of passage, and what lands on the windows blows across the glass like little rivers traveling by.

I was at the station in plenty of time for the six-forty.

Halt Ennery, the conductor, saw me climb aboard one of the coaches, and by the time we reached Creston, two hours late, he was ready for a break, so he slid into the seat next to me so we could chew the fat for a little while.

"Was that your train got shot at?" I asked by way of starting the conversation, though I already knew it'd been his.

"Wouldn't you know it?" he said. "Any misfortune or disaster waiting to happen along the Burlington Northern's waiting for my train."

"You don't want to start thinking that way. The next thing you know you'll be looking for the Jonah."

"Well, I've been keeping an eye on Laws Ruskell. I got my doubts about him."

"That's just because you two don't get along too well."

"I'm not saying it's his fault, mind. What I'm saying is some people are like lightning rods—they attract bad luck like magnets attract iron filings."

"You think the man who was shot in the head was that sort of lodestone?"

"Harold Chaney? I'd say anything but. There was a man with a golden touch. Throw him into a manure pile with a horseshoe in each hand and he'd come out of it riding a racehorse."

"You know him pretty good?"

"I knew him the way you'd know a friendly passenger who rode the train a lot. He always took a room, and when I'd stick my nose in he'd ask me to sit and chat a while. He even gave me a couple of tips on the futures market, but I talked it over with the wife and we decided better safe than sorry. He was a nice man who happened to have the gift of making money."

The way a lot of people in the Midwest still think about fame and fortune is that, first and foremost, you got to be a decent human being, a regular guy, one of the boys who maybe sits around the diner playing nickel poker and talking about the crops, who's not above coming to the dance at the Grange Hall on Saturday night and bringing along the little woman. They don't bother to think anybody who does that is doing something smart, something in his own interest, like that fella out in Indiana who cornered the soybean market one year with hardly a penny in his pocket to start, just because the farmers and elevator operators knew and liked him. A reputation for hard work is also useful, even if the hard work lasted two summers when you were just a boy. The thing is, you shouldn't be seen to be afraid of it, so when fame and fortune does finally drop into your lap it's seen as something you deserved.

"You ever meet his wife?"

"She traveled with him now and then, but I got the impression she'd rather take a plane for any trip over a hundred miles and only went along from time to time just to keep his temper sweet."

"He had a temper?"

"Well, how should I know?"

"You just said."

"That's just a way of speaking, Jake. You should know that."

"Well, I thought maybe you overheard an argument one time or another."

"I did, as a matter of fact."

"When was this?"

"Last time was about two weeks ago, if memory serves. Why? What's on your mind?" he asked, giving me the cocked eye.

"Nothing's on my mind. I just ask whatever question pops into my head."

"At random?"

"Well, no, not at random. One thing suggests another."

"What did I say that suggested Mr. Chaney and his wife had fights?"

"I didn't know they had fights. I asked if they had arguments now and then. You said he always took a room. You said she went along, pretty reluctant, now and then. So I figured if they argued there'd be nothing stopping them in the privacy of a room. Why do I have to tell you all this, Halt?"

"I like to know what's going on. How things work."

"All right. I'll satisfy you if and when I can, but I wonder could we just do it so I ask a few questions about this man who was killed and you answer them. I don't mind footnotes, but you keep going off along a spur leading nowhere, and first thing you know, you'll be popping up to do this and that and I'll be left with questions unanswered."

"You having a little indigestion?" Halt asked. "I got something for that in my bag."

"I'm okay. What were they fighting about two weeks ago?"

"Something she wanted to spend a lot of money on,

from the bits and pieces I overheard whilst passing by. He pointed out to her that his keystone company was under attack and it was no time to be throwing money around." He looked at his pocket watch, then, and stood up.

"Things to do, Jake," he said, and walked off just like I knew he'd do.

Eleven

THE FINANCIAL CENTER OF Chicago is around La Salle Street—the Midwest Stock Exchange—and West Jackson Boulevard, where you've got the MidAmerica Commodities Exchange, the Mercantile Exchange, the Options Exchange, and the Chicago Board of Trade right in a row.

The Options is in the Board of Trade's art-deco building with its three-story marble lobby.

Whenever I'm in town and have the time, I stop into the fifth-floor visitors' center where you can watch the action in The Pit. The frantic activity convinces me that my job suits me just fine, wandering around the plains on the trains, visiting my lady friends here and there, stopping by to chew the fat with old friends, with, every now and then, something exciting or challenging to add a little spice to life. The kind of excitement going on down on the Exchange floor wouldn't suit me at all.

I watched the traders for maybe fifteen minutes and

then I went looking for my friend Marcus Sears, who knows about as much about futures trading and Midwestern corporations as anyone I know. He's the chairman of the watchdog committee, doing a job similar to the one the SEC does for the New York Stock Exchange.

When his secretary announced me it was only half a minute before Marcus was out his office door and walking toward me with his hand outstretched.

He may be as old as eighty, but you'd never know it. His grip was like the grip of a man half his age, and when he led me back into his office he didn't lean on me any.

"You want something?" he asked. "I've got some Canadian rye as smooth as anything you can imagine."

"I'll have a finger."

He poured one for me into a highball glass so my nose would have the pleasure before my lips. I noticed that he didn't pour one for himself.

I raised an eyebrow when he handed me my glass.

He sat in the big leather chair behind a desk that was about a quarter of an acre of mahogany and poked his stomach with his finger.

"Doctor says no. Go ahead."

I took a sip and made the appropriate appreciative noises. He leaned back on the swivel and grinned with pleasure as though it was his own mouth and tongue getting the flavor.

"Sometimes I take a sip and just roll it around my mouth before I spit it out. Age is a thief, Jake."

"I can feel his hand in my pocket every now and then," I said.

"Visiting?" he asked.

"Railroad business."

"Harry Chaney?"

"I thought I'd ask you about him."

"According to the paper, they caught the boys who were shooting at the train. I suppose the authorities intend to treat it as a manslaughter, don't they? Damn-fool thing to do, but there doesn't seem to be any intent to murder Chaney."

"Well, no intent on the part of those young Indians."

"Like that, is it?"

"I don't know. I'm just looking."

"You want to know about Chaney," he said.

"Whatever you can tell me."

"The last ten years you'd call him an industrialist, maybe an entrepreneur, gathering up businesses, investing in new products, but he started thirty years ago right on the floor here. Started as a clerk for a trading firm. Wasn't long before he was trading on his own account."

"Good at it?"

"Uncommonly lucky, which is to say very good. You have to be lucky as well as smart to deal in futures if you're a speculator instead of a hedger."

I didn't say anything, which told him right away that I needed instruction.

"I don't know if I can make it simple," Marcus said.

"Well, if you see my eyes glaze over, you'll know it's not your whiskey, and you can go over that part again."

"All right. To begin with, you've got cash commitments—what the trader has to pay for the actual commodity, wheat, corn, oats, rye, soybeans, and so forth—and futures commitments. Trading provides insurance for the merchants and processors who actually handle and sell the goods.

"Say, for instance, a grain elevator operator buys wheat and stores it. At the same time he'll sell futures contracts for the same quantity. When the wheat is finally delivered, any change of price in the interval should have been canceled out by compensating changes in his cash and futures holdings.

"So far so good?"

"So far, I'm still on my feet."

"There're two theories about hedging. One is that inventory holders are insuring themselves against future price fluctuations by selling contracts for future delivery. The other says that hedging is done with the expectation of profit. Those're the arbitrageurs, taking advantage of a temporary price difference in two markets by buying in one and selling in the other.

"There are two kinds of hedgers. Short and long. Short hedgers have inventories and they sell futures contracts in like quantity. Long hedgers sell contracts on commodities not yet purchased."

"Sounds like betting both teams in a football game."

"There are similarities. If you could get a bet down for a hundred dollars on the Miami Dolphins at two to one, no points, and another on the Chicago Bears at two to one, no points, you couldn't lose."

"But the odds-makers would've already made the odds and everybody'd know them."

"Almost everybody. That's where inside trading and other illegalities figure in. But even in a well-regulated market, since the market is formed by conflicting opinion, there will always be a spread out of which a wily speculator can make a profit.

"Speculation is very risky, but when it pays off, it pays off hugely."

"That was Chaney?"

"In spades, doubled and redoubled. He made his bets and hardly ever lost."

"No suspicion that he was dealing seconds?"

"None at all. It was simply that Chaney was swift,

assured, and daring. Don't misunderstand. Sometimes he lost big, but he won big more than he lost. He was also smart enough to leave the wheel when he had his pile and invest his winnings in equities."

"Bought shares in companies."

"And became an important source of venture capital. Until he found his winner and ran with it."

"What winner would that be?"

"A process for pouring, drawing, shaping, and molding exotic alloys with enhanced electrical conductive properties."

"Those super-conductors I've been hearing about?"

"You mean the ones that need to be super-cooled? No. These are fragile amalgams that were short-lived until Lewis Warden turned up on Chaney's doorstep with a method of bonding and amalgamating that maintained these superior, desirable properties over a considerable span of time.

"Well, one thing led to another, and pretty soon the exotic alloys were only a small part of Chaney Enterprises, which is basically a group of companies dealing in exotic chemicals and rare metals."

"Who's their big customer?"

"Nearly everybody's big customer. The Pentagon."

"Figures."

"Defense and Space supports these technologies until entrepreneurs find applications in the consumer markets."

"Which Chaney did?"

"We're starting to cook with his products, eat off his ovenproof dishes, and use his machines in the hobby shops we've got in our basements. You want another finger of that rye?"

"I've had a sufficiency," I said, putting the glass on the leather-topped table at my elbow.

"It's a pity he should get shot when he was at the top

of his game. I don't think Chaney Enterprises will be able to resist now that he's gone."

"Resist what?"

"Take-over. When he saw the opportunities in the consumer markets he needed large amounts of capital for plant and expansion. So he went public and sold shares."

"Holding fifty-one percent for himself?"

"If you want to control a small company you might need fifty-one percent of the outstanding voting shares. But when you're dealing with a corporation as large as Chaney Enterprises, sometimes you can maintain effective control with as little as four or five percent. I'm sure Chaney personally held more than that, but I wouldn't know offhand how large his holdings were.

"I'm sure he could have gathered the proxies to allow him to refuse the tender offer, but now that he's dead, his partner and his wife might not have the skills or the means to make the fight."

"His partner? Lewis Warden?"

"Chaney could have played it otherwise but he's always been a fair man and made sure that Warden had a piece of the action even after his discoveries started playing a smaller and smaller part in the overall mix."

"Do you think it's possible Warden and Chaney's wife didn't want to make a fight of it? Maybe wanted the take-over to happen?"

"Are you calling that a motive?" Marcus said, jumping three squares ahead.

"I think it's worth putting it to the test."

I thanked Marcus and got ready to take my leave. He asked me if I'd like to join him for dinner and I said I didn't know how the rest of my day and evening was going to shape up.

"Well, I won't expect you, then, but if you can make it, I'll be at Binyon's in Plymouth Court. You know it?"

"I've been there."

"You have to put up with a lot of cigar-smoking lawyers, but I get a table over in the corner away from most of it, and they have the best turtle soup you've ever tasted."

Twelve

THE CHANEYS LIVED IN THE Gold Coast section of Chicago. Well, Harold Chaney used to live there and his widow still did, in a turn-of-the-century townhouse designed by Charles Palmer. It occupied a place of pride on Astor Street.

There was a painted iron jockey standing at the curb with his hand out holding an iron ring to which horses were once tethered. I noticed in passing that it had been repainted, not only the silks but the face and hands. Once they'd been black, and now were a pinkish white, proving to one and all that there was no prejudice in the Chaney household.

That didn't stop them from having a black to answer the door.

I'm pretty sure that he made more money than I did, but even so, he had to wear tuxedo pants, a black bow tie, and a white jacket, and I don't think I could've managed that.

He asked me what my business was with that

certain brand of snootiness that only the servants of the very rich ever use. That way people can be put off without it looking like the boss had any hand in it.

"My name's Jake Hatch. I met Mrs. Chaney at the morgue in Des Moines. I was in Chicago and I thought I'd stop by to see if I could be of any help."

"In exactly what way did you intend to be of help?" he asked.

"I don't exactly know. Suppose I ask the lady myself?"

"I've been authorized to convey any messages of condolence or offers of assistance."

"I don't want to get pushy," I said, "but instead of you making up her mind does she want to see me, why don't you go ask her while I wait here in the vestibule?"

She appeared at his back just at that minute.

"Charles?" she said, and he stepped aside like she'd pushed a button. "It's Mr. Hatch, isn't it?"

"Yes, ma'am," I said, taking off my hat.

"Did you wish to see me about something?"

"Oh, this isn't official. I was in town and thought I'd stop by and see if you arrived home safely. If you were all right."

"Kind of you. As you can see, I'm quite all right."

With Charles out of the way I stepped inside the house, saying, "If I keep you standing in a draft this way, you'll be sure to catch a cold. I remember when my father died. The doctor told me to keep an eye on my mother because people were especially susceptible to sickness in times of tragedy and distress."

Charles was watching her like a hawk. If she gave the nod I'm sure he would've done his best to hustle me out. But she seemed to make up her mind that it was better to let me have my look and get it over with than play games at the front door.

All of a sudden she turned on her heel and started toward the big double doors on one side of the entrance hall, which was as big as my whole flat back in Omaha.

"Charles. Tea and coffee. In the morning room."

The morning room wasn't a room used in the morning, I didn't think. It was a fancy living room. But I guess they had more than one, giving each one a different name. Like there probably was a morning room, a sitting room, a parlor, a library, a music room, and a living room, too.

There was a fire burning in a fireplace with an Adams mantelpiece. There were two short sofas in front of the hearth with a coffee table in between them. She sat on one of them and indicated that I was supposed to sit on the other.

She sat with her back straight, her knees close together slightly off to one side, her ankles crossed, and her hands lightly folded in her lap.

I didn't know how to sit, so I just sort of squatted on the edge of the chair like I didn't want to use up too much of it.

"This is very kind of you to inquire about my well-being," she said.

"Has your husband been brought back from Des Moines?"

"He's at the Adams-Winterfield Funeral Home."

"I don't know that one."

"It's in Downers Grove."

"Downers Grove must be twenty miles from the city."

"That's where Harold was born and raised. His mother still lives there in the old neighborhood. She's in her eighties. I wanted to make it as easy for her as I could."

"Is he going to be laid out?"

"I'd rather he wasn't, but she wanted it. The old ways die hard with some people. But the casket will be closed."

"Well, if you wanted to press it, the custom is that the wife has first claim."

"If she wants it."

"When's the funeral to be?"

"I prevailed so far as that was concerned. It will only be the immediate family and a few—a very few—friends attending a brief ceremony in the funeral chapel in two days' time. Cremation to follow."

"An important man like your husband'll have a lot of friends and associates that'll want to pay their respects."

"They can drive out to Downers Grove and sign the visitors' book or they can attend the memorial service being arranged in the chapel at the Chicago Board of Trade."

Charles came wheeling in a serving cart big enough to hold three pots, two cups and saucers, a sugar bowl, cream pitcher, a saucer of lemon wedges, the necessary silverware, a rose in a silver bud vase, and a three-tiered plate of buttered bread and cookies.

After Charles had left and Mrs. Chaney had poured tea for herself and coffee for me, I said, "Mrs. Chaney, are you completely satisfied that your husband's death was an accident?"

She looked at me as though I'd made a mildly interesting remark about the weather.

"Aren't you?"

"No, I'm not."

"On what evidence?"

"No evidence I can lay my hand on and hold up to the light."

"Well?" she said, her voice as light as a feather and remote as a moonbeam.

"Did your husband have any particular enemies?"

The silvery laugh that broke from her lips nearly made me drop my cup.

"I'm sorry, Mrs. Chaney. Are you all right?"

She recovered right off and brushed a handkerchief across her mouth. I had the feeling she was working me.

"Coming from a policeman . . ."

"Railroad detective, ma'am."

". . . your question startled me. Yes. Railroad detective. I'm sure that informs you about the ways of the world. A man doesn't make the success my husband made without making a great many enemies along the way."

"I understand that theory as an abstraction, but making enemies of business rivals isn't exactly what I had in mind. I was thinking of somebody he might've hurt bad enough to grow the will to kill him or have him killed."

She stared at me for half a minute, then turned her head to stare into the fire. I let her have the time. When she looked at me again there was a certain solemnness to her manner.

"Have you asked that question often in your career, Mr. Hatch?"

"Often enough."

"And do people really begin to recite lists of possible murderers?"

"No, but they sometimes name names of people they think might have done it."

"And have any ever proved to have done it?"

"More than once."

"All right, then. Milton Banner, my husband's ex–brother-in-law."

"Mr. Chaney was married before?"

"He was married when young to Elizabeth Banner. They had two children and were together for ten years before she died. When I met Harold he was already well-off but not yet wealthy. He'd made a considerable amount of money but was just entering upon the enterprises that were to make his fortune. There were difficult times the first year or two. It always looks as though successful men have more than they really do. Nearly everything was mortgaged. He was deeply in debt. He was a man obsessed by business and ambition, desperately in need of affection, companionship, and someone to care for his neglected children."

"Why would Mr. Banner have it in for your husband?"

"They had been associated in some of Harold's dealings. When he was ready to try for the top, he didn't want Milt along."

"Why was that?"

"Have you ever climbed a mountain, Mr. Hatch?"

"No, ma'am, I haven't."

"I was in a party climbing Huascarán in Peru. Twenty-two thousand feet. Not the most difficult climb, but I wasn't in perfect condition. Hadn't trained for it enough. So I was left behind when they made the assault on the summit. It's not that they didn't like me, or appreciate me for my other qualities, it was just that they didn't want to risk it. I could have faltered and made us all fail."

"So Mr. Chaney was the sort of man who wouldn't try to carry anybody who couldn't cut it?"

"That's the only way to be when you're going for the summit."

"Is Mr. Banner your only candidate?"

She hesitated and finally said, "Terry Pickering, perhaps. He has a cruel temper. Harold and Terry went head to head over something a while ago and have hated one another ever since."

"What was the something?"

"Me."

"Anybody else?"

"Assorted fools and madmen without number." She turned her head toward the doorway before I could reply. I didn't see her do it, but she must've pressed a bell push under the carpet near her foot, because Charles was standing there.

"That's all I can tell you, Mr. Hatch," she said, getting to her feet.

"I hope you don't mind if I stop by again."

"What for?"

"In case any new questions come to mind."

"May I ask you a question, Mr. Hatch?"

"Ma'am?"

"Are you authorized to go around investigating an accident like you're doing? Is it within your jurisdiction?"

"Not exactly," I said. "If they go ahead with an inquiry, it'll probably be run by someone from the state police or the attorney general's office."

"Well, why don't you just let them get on with it if they want to?" she said, sweetly.

She picked up a magazine off the coffee table, letting me know she didn't expect any reply, and before I knew it, I was at the door with Charles waiting for me to leave.

"Say, didn't I see Mrs. Chaney in the theater or on television, maybe?"

"Some years ago, I do believe Mrs. Chaney pursued a dramatic career," Charles said.

"I was wondering about one more thing," I said, as he started closing the door, my cue to get the hell out of the doorway. "Was Mrs. Chaney having a birthday soon?"

He just fish-eyed me.

"Or maybe the Chaneys were having an anniversary?"

"No birthday, no anniversary, and no other holiday of consequence," Charlie said, telling me to mind my own business.

So no reason for a five-carat emerald unless Chaney was the sort of man who gave such gifts to his wife on a whim.

Thirteen

THERE WAS NO BEST person to question next.

I'd meant to ask Florence Chaney where her husband's ex–brother-in-law could be found, but I didn't bother going back to find out because I had an idea she wouldn't have bothered to keep track of him.

I had a notion that Milton Banner would take the opportunity to gloat over the brother-in-law who'd left him behind while he went on to make millions. The proper place for such gloating would be the funeral home where Chaney was laid out.

I checked with the Adams-Winterfield receptionist on the telephone and was told that Harold Chaney was, indeed, in a slumber room prepared for visitors starting that night and did I know the coffin was closed.

I got over there by cab just after nightfall. There was a little slotted board with white plastic letters directing people to the different rooms where the deceased were waiting for their guests.

I stepped into the room occupied by Harold Chaney. I assumed he was in the huge mahogany casket, almost buried in banks of flowers, sitting at the back of the room in front of windows draped in burgundy velvet.

The coffin was closed, just like I'd been told. I doubted any sort of reconstruction of his face and head would've been possible, certainly not in any practical length of time. Instead there was a sixteen-by-twenty photograph of the dead man placed on top of the lid in a silver frame.

There was a woman seated in a love seat off to one side, her head turned away from the casket. The fingers of a small gloved hand clutching a handkerchief were touching her chin. A nearby lamp threw light on her face. She looked young, like an actress dressed up in the style of an old woman. Then she moved her head and I saw the age wasn't makeup, it was real, every eighty-some years of it.

There was a middle-aged black woman, wearing a black cloth coat unbuttoned over a white uniform, sitting one seat behind and one seat over. She was wearing nurse's shoes. The old woman coughed and the nurse leaned forward with real concern in her eyes.

Neither one had seen me yet. The carpet was so thick I hadn't made a sound coming in. I walked up to the coffin and knelt down on the prayer bench.

I have no faith myself, but I always say a few words for the dead person whenever I attend one of these things.

Up close I could see from the photograph that Harold Chaney had been a very good-looking man. If he'd been an actor instead of a successful entrepreneur and industrialist, he'd've always been cast as a successful entrepreneur and industrialist. I got up and placed my hand on the lid. It was warm to the touch. Then I went over to old Mrs. Chaney, bending over and taking the hand she offered me.

"I'm sorry for your troubles," I murmured, in the way the Irish used to offer condolences when she'd been young and me younger still.

Her fingers tightened on mine. I think she remembered how it was when people expressed themselves that way, too.

"Were you a business associate of my son's?"

"No, ma'am, I never even had the pleasure of meeting him."

A little frown appeared between her eyes, but when I tried to take my hand away she wouldn't let go.

"Why are you here, then?"

"I'm with the railroad."

The frown deepened and she coughed again. The nurse leaned forward and said, "Should we go home and come back again in maybe an hour? It's almost supper time and people—"

"No, no, Maddy. I want to sit here when it's quiet. I want to sit here with my son when a lot of people aren't hovering around me or sitting on the folding chairs staring at a closed box."

"You want a lozenge, then?"

"Maybe a little water, please, Maddy."

When Maddy slid out to go fetch the water, old Mrs. Chaney squeezed my hand again and told me to sit down beside her.

"Have you been sent to show respect or to make sure none of us related to him are thinking about suing Amtrak for carelessness and neglect?"

"I'm employed by the Burlington Northern."

"Well, we might sue them too," she said, finally letting go of my hand. She smiled and looked at the coffin again. "There was a time Harold might have done. If it was me or Elizabeth who got shot in the head while at supper in the dining car. He could have used the money once upon a time."

"Elizabeth?"

"His first wife. The mother of his children. She didn't live to enjoy the fruits of all their labor. Why am I telling you all this?"

"I'm not here spying for the railroad."

"What, then?"

"I'm a detective."

She straightened up and moved back a couple of inches as though trying to get a better look at me.

"You don't look like a detective."

"What's a detective supposed to look like?"

"I don't know, but not you. You look like a milkman."

"Who delivers milk anymore?"

"No one. You look like a milkman the way a milkman used to look. But you say you're a detective and I believe you. So what are you doing here?"

"I thought maybe I could sit over to the other side there and read faces."

"Looking for what? Signs of guilty pleasure?"

"It doesn't bother you there might be people coming here that'll be glad your son's dead?"

"What's your name?" she asked.

"Jake Hatch."

"Well, Jake, I can't imagine anyone, man or woman, living life with any vigor or intent to achieve, that won't collect some envy, jealousy, and anger against them by the time they die. Who did you have in mind?"

"Milton Banner."

"Who told you Milton would be glad my Harold was shot?"

"Your daughter-in-law."

"You mean Florence?"

"Isn't she your daughter-in-law?"

"Marriage made her so. I never considered her so. I loved my Harold's first wife. It's possible that losing her so young made it hard for me to ever favor any other woman Harold took up with. But I don't think so. I think I don't like Florence because Florence isn't likable. Not to women."

"Why would she tell me that Milton hated your son?"

"Possibly because she didn't like Milton. He was one of the few men who didn't fall for her. Did you fall for her?"

"No, ma'am."

"That's good," she said, patting my hand, looking at her hand as she did so. I could see the bulge of rings under the gloves.

"You ever wonder why old women wear gloves?" she asked.

"Keep their fingers warm? Hide their jewelry?" I said, trying to make a little joke.

She stripped off one glove. She had rings on every finger except the thumb and pinkie.

"No," she said. "Because it's the only part of their body they can't help looking at. I mean your hands are out there flailing around, aren't they? No way to avoid looking at them, reminding you of how old you are. So you cover them with gloves. Think about it."

I wanted to get her back onto her present daughter-in-law, the one she didn't like.

"So you're saying that Mrs. Chaney—"

"Florence. Don't want you to mix us up."

"You saying that Florence wanted to cause Milton some mischief?"

"I don't know what she could do to him that life hasn't already done. Milton's as mild as milk. Doesn't have the ambition of a turtle and never did. My son and Milton were in a few arrangements together. I think Harold sort of dragged Milton into these things because Elizabeth's folks had hopes that Harold's good example would build a fire under Milton. It didn't. Milton wanted to do what he was doing."

"What was that?"

"Odd jobs. Selling peanuts at the stadium in summer, hot dogs at the ice-skating rink in winter, whatever. He didn't want or need much. He wasn't married. Didn't even have a girlfriend. Liked to go to the movies and have a few beers in some neighborhood tavern. Liked to paint pictures. Liked to go hunting. That was his biggest extravagance, I suppose. Going hunting as often as he could."

"So it was no loss to him when Harold decided he was in a race and Milton couldn't keep up?"

"I was there when Milton told Harold he'd had enough of business."

Maddy came back with the glass of water. Old Mrs. Chaney thanked her, took a sip, and handed it back.

"People coming," Maddy said, gesturing with her chin.

"If Milton stops by, I'd like to talk to him," I said. "If it's all right with you, I'll just sit back there in the corner. If he comes in, will you give me the nod?"

She thought about that for about fifteen seconds, studying my face to see if she could trust me not to do inoffensive people any harm. Then she patted my hand and nodded just as a woman nearly her age came whispering over with her face set in the sadness of a hound.

Very quickly I rubbed my thumb across her rings and made another little joke. "I see rubies and I see diamonds, but no emeralds."

"Hate emeralds," she said, just as the woman took her hand from me.

"Anybody in your family have the initials PIP?"

Tears popped into her eyes like a magic trick.

"Not initials. A name. He called his first wife—he called Elizabeth—Pip. Where did you hear it?"

"I don't think I heard it. I think I saw it written down somewhere. Maybe in your son's bedroom on the train," I lied. "Did he ever call your granddaughter or anybody else Pip?"

"Never."

I found the last chair in the last row in the back of the room. For an hour I watched all sorts of people stopping to pay their respects.

The longer I sat there, the more I got the feeling that whoever killed him or had him killed would be right there in the room with me, which was not to say the guilty party would come strolling in wearing a sign.

It was warm in the room and the smell of the flowers was heavy.

Fourteen

I WAS SHOVED OUT of a dream in which five or six of my lady friends, widowed, divorced, or never married—mature women who should have learned a thing or two about the benefits and disadvantages of that institution—were all pushing me out the door, telling me it was time to accept the responsibilities society puts upon us. To stop thrashing around and accept the harness God meant us all to wear, pulling the load of life in tandem.

When I opened my eyes, Maddy was nudging my shoulder, staring at me wide-eyed, as though hoping I wouldn't come out of my doze with a shout and make a scandal.

"Remind me never to hire you to watch the barn," she said.

I said, "What?," which was about all I was capable of saying.

"Mr. Banner's here," she said.

"Where?"

"I think he went down to the smoking room."

"Did he go up to the casket and pay his respects?"

"He went up and stared at it for a long time, but he didn't kneel to say a prayer."

"Well, not everybody does."

She made a mouth that said she couldn't understand people without common piety and went back to sit behind Mrs. Chaney. It was then I noticed that Florence Chaney was sitting in the first row with a young man in his twenties sitting next to her. A young woman around the same age, with carroty-red hair, was sitting next to old Mrs. Chaney. I assumed it was the granddaughter and that the young man was the grandson.

I slipped out of my seat and went out into the lobby. There was a staircase at the back leading down. Two little signs on the wall directed people to the rest rooms and a smoking lounge.

I went down two flights. The carpet on the lower stairway was worn pretty thin, proving the old business proposition of putting your money up front where it could be seen.

There was only one person in the smoking room. It had to be Milton. He had the slightly run-over look of a man in mid-life who'd never made it and was struggling to make ends meet when most men at least had a more or less comfortable home, some money in the bank, and—except for unpersuaded men like me—a grown-up family who cared about them. What he didn't have was the worried look most men his age have that whatever they've accomplished could be wiped away, just like that, by some catastrophe.

He was bending over with his elbows on his knees, staring at the cigarette he was smoking, as though aware that it was an unacceptable indulgence but one which he sadly realized he could not do without.

When he looked at me I could see he had the eyes of

a dreamer, but one who had no firm grasp on any particular dream.

"You here to see Harold Chaney?" I asked.

"Well, he can't be seen, can he?" he said in a very soft voice. "He's boxed up for burning."

"Is he going to be cremated?" I asked.

"Hell of a waste, isn't it?"

"That fancy mahogany casket?"

"I'll bet it cost five thousand dollars. Do you suppose they actually burn something that expensive or do they take the dear departed out of the showpiece and put him in a paper bag before sliding him into the fire?"

"I suppose there's a law against it."

"Well, I suppose so, too. Even so. You could panel part of a room or make a nice chair out of the wood."

I sat down in the chair next to him.

"You a friend of Harold's?" he asked.

"No. My name's Jake Hatch. I work for the railroad on which Mr. Chaney was killed."

"My name's Milton Banner," he said, holding out his hand as though he expected this was going to be the beginning of a long friendship.

"Mr. Chaney's brother-in-law?"

"Ex. I was his brother-in-law as long as my sister was alive."

"I suppose that once a person's an in-law through marriage, death or divorce doesn't change that status, would you say?"

"Fine point of custom?" he asked himself as well as me.

"So you knew him pretty well while he was getting started?"

"He was going to be the salvation of me," Banner said. "That was the hope."

"Whose hope?"

"The hope of my folks. I was no longer the bumptious boy when my sister married Harold. I was a man too long grown to be doing what I was doing."

"What was that?"

"Practically nothing, according to my folks. Odd jobs to keep myself in a room and feed myself while I painted."

"You still painting?"

"Oh, yes. Painting and hunting're the only things ever interested me in life. You think they make a funny pair?"

"How's that?"

"Well, painting's a gentle pastime and hunting's violent."

"I don't know that artists have always been nonviolent people."

"The question is, am I a violent person?"

When I looked at him, he had his head turned and was looking up at me with a little smile on his face. Then he straightened up and put his cigarette out in the ashtray on the table next to him.

We sat there grinning at each other.

"I know you from somewhere else?" I asked.

"If we'd ever met before, you'd have remembered. I don't think you're the sort who forgets much. It doesn't take a mental whiz to figure out you came down here looking for me and knew who I was when you walked through the door. Question is, who are you?"

"I told you. My name's Jake Hatch and I work for the Burlington Northern."

"Railroad detective?"

"That's right."

"What's your interest?"

"I'd like to know if it was a random shot that killed your brother-in-law."

"You think I hid out there in the tulles and waited

for the train to come by just as Harold was sitting down to dinner and blew his head off through the window?"

"It could have been done."

"Only if somebody was a mind reader. Who'd know he was going to sit down just about that time?"

"That's a good question." I took out my notebook and wrote it down. "I'm not as good remembering things as you may think."

"Mine's starting to fade, I can tell you that."

The one thing that surely never fades is feelings of strong hate and the desire for revenge. All I had to do was find out if there was anything strong enough between Chaney and Banner to warrant killing ten years after their relationship had ended.

"You come to see Harold to refresh your memory about something?"

"Oh, my, you mean like did I hate Harold for dropping me by the wayside?"

"It's a thought."

"I liked Harold. I didn't love him like a brother, even when we were together sometime during practically every day. What we wanted out of life was too much different to make us close friends. But I liked him and never wished him any harm."

"Even when he dumped you and went on to make a fortune?"

"I never wanted a fortune. You're as bad as my folks used to be. They just couldn't understand that I didn't want a fortune. I never wanted to pay the price. Not because I had dreams of being a great artist. I was never good enough to be anything but passable. But it gave me joy and it's all I ever wanted."

"That and hunting."

He shrugged, having said all he was going to say about that.

"Besides, Harold didn't do me rotten. He gave me

some shares in the parent company before it started to grow all over the place."

Something in my expression must have asked the question, because he made a great show of looking down at his run-over shoes and brushing off the front of his jacket.

"Even a few shares in such a successful enterprise should allow me to keep up appearances a little better than this, right?"

"Well, I . . ."

"Even if artists are supposed to be careless about how they dress, surely even they would spruce up for a funeral if they had the means to do so, right?"

I didn't bother even starting a comment.

"I sold off the shares he gave me one by one—usually at the bottom of a market—and I don't have but a very few left. The dividends each half don't count for much."

"You could sell them too, couldn't you?"

"I could, but I was finally acting with a little bit of prudence. I was holding them until Chaney Enterprises was bought up by the Whente Conglomerate."

"Oh? That's the first I heard who was behind it."

"You follow the financial world pretty carefully, do you?" he asked, smirking at me.

"I was just responding. You know. I thought it was better than saying huh."

I was beginning to see that Banner wasn't a very likable fella. The bohemian pretensions that might be attractive in a young man soon wear thin as the years go on. Pretty soon failure gets bigger than aspiration. When there's no payoff, it's no longer possible to admire somebody living on hope and doubtful expectations, even if a few do get famous after they're dead. Most failed artists aren't admired and become bitter people, too late wanting what they never gave time to earn.

"Is Chaney's death going to affect the deal?" I asked.

He shrugged. "I wouldn't know. I don't sit in on the board meetings. I expect Florence Chaney and the two children will own the majority of the voting shares."

"Not the grandmother?"

"Harold provided for her long ago. I doubt he would've based the money that guarantees her security on stocks in his own firm. He used to tell me stories how old people with such holdings were bilked and cheated out of them if anything happened to the original management. Her fortune's all in municipals and treasury bonds, I'll bet."

"Does Florence Chaney know enough about the business to make the right decision?"

"That depends on who you ask about what the right decision might be. I was all for the buy-out because it would've increased the value of the few shares I've got left. Lewis Warden might not be for it."

"Chaney's partner?"

"And executive assistant. He's a fairly young man and he'd probably rather have the companies to run than the small fortune he'd realize from his own shares if the deal went through."

"How young is young?"

"Late thirties. He was the metallurgy whiz that started the whole shebang. But I hear tell he's as interested in management and administration as metallurgy since the corporation expanded."

"Is he a social friend of the Chaneys besides being a business associate?"

He gave me that sly, sarcastic grin.

"Very friendly. Very friendly," he said.

Fifteen

CHICAGO TO DENVER is one thousand and thirty-eight railroad miles, an overnighter, and Chaney was not the sort of man to ride the coaches. In fact, it was a wonder to me that a man with his money, who was known to love the trains so much, didn't have a private car ready to be hooked up for his frequent trips from one city to another.

I checked with reservations, where sleeper patrons are recorded by name, and saw that Chaney'd made the journey over the past year and a half at least once a week and sometimes more.

If I asked anybody, I already knew what they'd say, that Chaney's business took him all over the place and when I asked how come so much to Denver they'd say they didn't know but surely it had to be on business. After all, he had plants and factories all along the way.

I found out for a fact that his pilot plant, where all the new products and manufacturing techniques were tested, was in Fort Morgan, Colorado, and since I was told that was where this Lewis Warden could be found most of the time, I decided that was going to be the next place I'd visit.

Fort Morgan was only thirty-four miles from Akron, where my friends Bess and George McGilvray lived.

Also, Maggie Wister, who'd helped me on a case not long ago, because she was deaf and mute and could read lips, had her little house about a half dozen miles outside of Akron along a country road. A calmer, sweeter woman you'll never meet, and it had been a month or more since I'd paid a visit.

The train took me into Fort Morgan at six-fifteen in the morning. I called Janel Butterfield, who lived about fifteen miles outside of town, and asked her if she'd welcome a visit and she said she would after only a moment's hesitation.

Janel puts the most delicious country breakfast you ever tasted on the table. The eggs are fresh out of the hen house, the ham sliced from quarters she's smoked herself with hickory and applewood, the honey comes from her own hives, the bees browsing clover and fruit trees, and the milk is the real stuff, traded with a farmer down the road who swears Janel bakes the best sweet rolls in the state.

I borrowed a ride with the postman who drives out to the end of his rural route and works back. Janel's nearly at the beginning of it, so it was no time at all before I was sitting down to ambrosia while Janel sat across the table from me in the sunshine coming through the kitchen window and studied me in a way that made me a little uncomfortable.

"What is it, Janel?" I asked. "Is there something different about me?"

"How old are you now, Jake?"

"Well, now, Janel," I said, somewhat startled, "I've never known you to ask a personal question like that."

"You're fifty-five if you're a day."

"Well, all right, that's close enough so's not to matter."

"It's time to stop larking about."

"Larking? What do you mean, larking, Janel?"

"I mean visiting a woman in every train station along the way. Even some that have been taken off the timetable. Like Akron, for instance."

"Akron, Ohio?"

"You know very well I mean Akron, Colorado, where a widow by the name of Maggie Wister lives."

"Maggie Wister?"

"The lady who's deaf and dumb."

"Mute, Janel. They don't say dumb anymore. It's got connotations."

Janel dipped her head. "Thank you. I'll remember that. Of course I never used the word to Mrs. Wister."

"You've talked to her?" I blurted out, wondering what was going on here.

"I've got a cousin lives outside of Akron."

"I didn't know."

A little smile curled up one side of Janel's pretty mouth. "Well, maybe I didn't mention my cousin because she's a pretty divorcee."

"I see," I said, just to have something to say and give myself some thinking room.

"We went to a social at her church one Sunday afternoon. Maggie Wister was there. She's a very nice woman."

"Yes, she is."

"Suffers her widowhood in quiet."

"Well, she'd have to, wouldn't she?"

"That's not a joke, is it, Jake? I don't think being deaf is something to joke about."

"It wasn't meant as a joke. It was just an observation. But I might mention that Maggie Wister takes it more lightly than you're taking it if I do say something amusing about her condition."

"Women put up with a lot when a man is decent otherwise and they think there's hope."

"Hope for what, Janel?"

"Hope for getting married, Jake."

"Oh."

"How many years have you been grazing in one meadow and then another?"

I kind of liked the way Janel put my amorous adventures into pastoral terms.

"I'm not sure I get your meaning."

"How many years have you been romancing a dozen ladies at a time?"

"No, no, not a dozen. Please."

She was embarrassing me and it was hard for me to respond modestly in the face of the facts.

"However many. How many years?"

"Well, I've had several lady friends for as long as I can remember. A man can live solitary with reasonable contentment, but there are times when he misses simple things like hugging a woman something awful."

"A woman can live solitary too, Jake. Maybe we can do it a lot better than men. After all, we know, married or not, we'll probably live our last years out all alone, children grown and gone, husband dead or gone off with a younger woman."

"Oh dear," I said.

"What are you oh-dearing about?"

"You're not going to scold me for every man that ever left a wife, are you, Janel?"

"Of course not. I'm going to scold you for wanting to be the everlasting boy. You've got too much of a pot . . ."

"Hey!"

". . . to be playing Peter Pan. You've got to stop flitting from flower to flower. You've got to settle on one."

"Just a minute, Janel," I said, "I don't mind a little lecture with my hot cakes, but it seems to me I have a perfect right to live my life the way I want to."

"I never said you didn't. What I'm saying is you've got to face the realities."

"What realities?"

"We're coming into the plague years, just as it's written in the Bible. Don't make a face at me. You know I'm a believer but no fanatic. Bible or no, the plague years are upon us. You can believe they're punishment for the promiscuity that ran riot in the world over the last ten or twenty years, or you can believe they're not, but you can't not believe there's some connection with what's happening now and what went before. Forget about divine punishment. Just look at the data. Everybody dies who gets the plague, sooner or later, and the kind of gallivanting you've been used to makes you a candidate."

"Now, just hold on a minute here," I said. *She'd started to scare me.* "You've got me in my coffin."

"I've got you in danger. In danger of getting it and in danger of passing it around."

"Now you're making me sound like the Typhoid Mary of AIDS. I don't seek or enjoy the company of ladies who're likely to have it."

"You have a friend, Harriet Lawry, in Denver?"

I was beginning to like this less and less. It looked to me like Janel, and maybe others, were checking up on me more than was right or a whole crowd of my women acquaintances were networking and comparing notes on me.

"How do you know Harriet Lawry? Was she at the church social too?"

"Never mind," she said, waving any further questions away. "Ms. Lawry's an artist, isn't she?"

"You're not going to tell me now that artists are more promiscuous than most."

"I'm saying that she's an attractive woman, from what I've heard, and you certainly don't flatter yourself that you're her only friend, do you? If she seeks the company of others, maybe artists like herself, painters and writers and musicians, the first thing you know you're coming awfully close to drug users and bisexual men in greater numbers than you'd find in the ordinary population."

"You can't go condemning a whole class of people—"

"I'm not condemning. I'm not accusing. I'm simply saying the odds of passing around the virus increases in big cities and among certain people. For the good Lord's sake, Jake, I'm not making judgments. I've been generous enough with my favors not to claim sainthood. I'm just saying times have changed and you can't keep playing the ram amid the flock anymore."

All this lecturing didn't do a lot of good to my appetite, and then there was that crack about my pot. So I only went back for seconds instead of thirds and didn't put any cream in my fourth cup of coffee.

Then I thanked Janel sweetly, kissed her on the mouth with minimal body contact—because I knew she'd only say no to anything I might suggest anyway—and told her I'd think about what she'd said on my way back to town.

"How do you expect to get there?" she asked.

"I expect I'll catch a ride with somebody on their way in."

"I doubt it," she said. "Let me get my coat and I'll

drive you in. I have things to buy at the market anyway."

Which is what we did. I kissed her again in Fort Morgan, on the cheek this time, and went to the drugstore to call the factory to see if Lewis Warden was there.

Sixteen

Lewis Warden was waiting for me in his office. As expected, he was the same Lewis who'd shown up at the morgue in Des Moines with Mrs. Chaney. But I hadn't seen him the first evening at the funeral home.

He was sitting behind a desk that looked like a made-over laboratory table. The outlet cut into the top for a Bunsen burner was still there off in one corner. There was another such workbench with a rack for test tubes and retorts against one wall. There was no carpet on the floor. Instead it was surfaced with rubber industrial matting. About the only things that made the room look like anything but a working lab was a lawyer's bookcase behind and to one side of his desk. It was filled with marksmanship trophies and more were displayed on the top.

"You're pretty good?" I said.

"Not Olympic class, but world class," he said. "I went into training for the winter biathlon about eight years ago but it took too much time away from my work."

"Which is metallurgy?"

"Specifically, the plating, molding, and drawing of exotic alloys."

He took a packet of chewing gum from his sweater pocket and offered me a stick. I said no, it got caught in my partial. He unwrapped a stick, folded it twice, and popped it into his mouth.

"Winter biathlon's what? Riding, fencing . . ." I started to ask.

"It's a twenty-kilometer cross-country race on skis with firing exercises with a rifle at four, eight, twelve, and sixteen kilometers."

"You do any other kind of shooting?"

"A little bench and skeet. Are you a gun enthusiast, Mr. Hatch?"

"Well, no. I'm a pretty good offhand shot, of course. Any man raised out in the country as a boy has shot himself a squirrel or two, maybe a deer."

"Did you shoot your deer?"

"That's what decided me against hunting. I got me a buck when I was twelve. I can still plink a tin can at thirty yards nine times out of ten, but I get no pleasure from it."

"Anybody who likes guns is a nut, that it?"

"I never said that. No, to each his own, I always say. Anybody wants to plink away at clay birds and paper targets, that's okay with me. Shooting animals and people? Now that's a different thing. You ever shoot animals?"

"Now and then."

"What about people?"

"Not lately."

"How's that, not lately?"

"I did my tour in Nam."

I nodded.

"You ever do a tour?" he asked.

"Korea was my war," I said.

"Police action."

"Whatever. People were dying, no matter what they called it."

"See any combat?" he asked.

"Saw plenty but wasn't in it. CID."

"So you got a taste of being a cop in the Criminal Investigation Division?" he said.

"Oh, I think I would've ended up being a cop anyway. My mother always said I was a nosy one even when I was knee-high."

"So, is it just being nosy that's got you looking into Harold's accident?"

"You're convinced of that, are you?"

"They've got those Indians in the slammer up in Marshalltown and—"

"How's that?" I asked, busting right in on him. "When I went to see those young men they were in the jail at Indianola."

"I expect they didn't think that little lockup would hold them if they decided to break out."

"Why would they want to break out?"

"To avoid trial, I suppose," Warden said, frowning as though I was irritating him with all these foolish questions. "State's attorney's office is bringing charges of manslaughter."

"Involuntary?"

"Not that I heard. It'll be on the news tonight and in the papers by morning. I hear that the attorney general intends to prosecute to the limit and ask for the max."

"On all six of them? Some of those youngsters are underage."

He shrugged his shoulders and tossed a pill of silver

paper torn from the gum wrapper at the Bunsen burner hole and scored a hit.

"Where'd you hear all this?"

"I naturally called the capital to find out what they intended doing. Harold Chaney was an important man in this state. It seems a crying shame he had to die because a bunch of beered-up Indians decided to use a train for a moving target."

He tossed another pill, and scored another hit.

"I didn't see you at the funeral home last night," I said.

"I'll be there tonight," he said.

"How come you waited?"

"I was here and the funeral home's in Chicago."

"That's what I mean. How come you were here? How come you didn't go back to Chicago with Mrs. Chaney after you escorted her to the morgue in Des Moines?"

"This company's in the middle of a take-over attempt. Somebody had to be here at headquarters minding the store."

"I thought headquarters was back in Chicago."

"The main business and sales offices are there. But the heart of Chaney Enterprises is right here."

I got up as though my business with him was finished.

"Was Harold Chaney for or against the take-over of his company?" I suddenly asked.

I thought Warden hesitated for a second before he got to his feet and said, "Against it, naturally. Harry wasn't ready for retirement yet. He had plenty of ambition and energy left in him."

I stuck out my hand and shook his, wondering how come it was sometimes people would call a friend or associate by his given name, then by a nickname, and when did they use one or the other.

"Oh, just one other thing," I said when I'd reached the door.

"What's that?"

"Where were you around the time Harold Chaney was shot?"

"Dinner time? I guess I was at home having my own supper. I must've been at home because that's where Florence found me after she got the news."

"Home? I never did ask you where you lived, did I? Not Chicago?"

"Nearer here than there," he said. "My home is the same one I was born and grew up in. Right here in Fort Morgan."

"Almost a thousand miles from Chicago," I said.

"And almost seven hundred to Ottumwa," he said, rolling up another pill and making another bull's-eye. "I was home having supper, and that's where Florence got me first time when she called about nine o'clock."

He was telling me he could never have traveled fourteen hundred miles, seven hundred each way, in about two hours. I didn't point out that he could've been in Ottumwa with no trouble if he and Florence Chaney had reason to lie for one another.

Seventeen

I TOOK THE BUS, rode the thirty-four miles into Akron, and went over to the sheriff's office.

George McGilvray was in his office with his feet up on the desk, staring at the map of the county on the wall. He thumped his boot heels on the floor as he reached out to take my hand.

McGilvray's no rural county sheriff even if Washington County isn't that populated. He was a captain of police in Denver for over twenty years and only pinned on a badge again because old man Chickering dropped dead of a heart attack and there was no one else willing to take on the job.

"How've you been keeping, Jake?" he asked.

"I've been under siege," I said.

"How's that?"

"Every woman I know has decided it's time for them to settle down into a monogamous relationship."

"Understandable, considering all the press and television this AIDS has been getting."

"You think it's how morals were invented? Nothing to do with abstractions of the spirit but practical rules for survival?"

"I'd say it was likely, though I'd also say that whoever decides these things was going too far sending a plague just to get Jake Hatch married."

I made a whoosh of disdain for his lame attempt at humor and asked how his Bess was keeping.

"The arthritis seems to have let up a little lately. Her hands are a pity to look at, but she says they don't pain her as much." He looked up at the wall clock. "I could leave early if you wanted to come back to the house with me."

"I'm afoot, so you'd have to drive me back again."

"Maybe you'll stay the night," he said. "We'll see."

Bess was at the back porch sweeping out the kitchen and mud room when we pulled into the back yard. Her old station wagon was sitting off to one side gathering dust, so I had an idea she wasn't driving it much because her arthritis was hurting her more than she wanted to let on.

She put aside her broom and gave me a hug.

"Come on in, Jake. We've missed you."

George put his hand on my back and urged me through the doors into the big old-fashioned kitchen with the stove against one wall and the table in the middle of the floor close to its heat in the winter and next to the opposite wall underneath the window to catch the breeze in summer. It was spring, the days and nights sometimes hot and sometimes cold, so it sat there in the middle of the linoleum just in case, even though the afternoon was warm.

"If this was England it'd be time for tea," Bess said, "so sit down and I'll make us a cup."

George and I settled down around the table while she fussed with the tea, George tossing a glance her way every now and then, wanting to take the kettle and pot from her, but knowing she'd object.

"I read about the accident," George said.

"They're going to bring those Indians to trial for manslaughter," I said.

He said the same thing I'd said when Warden mentioned it. "Involuntary?"

"I don't know how the charge will come down, but they mean to make an example out of them."

"Well, I suppose it's right. If they killed a man through their carelessness, they should pay the price."

"I think they'll be paying a price for something they didn't do. At least most of them will."

"How's that?"

I started telling them the story from the beginning, mentioning the distance from which the shooting took place, the hole in the first window, the condition of the head after the bullet had done with it and the window blown out on the other side, and what Catalina had to say about all of that.

"Sounds like she's right to me," George said. "Hunting rifle with soft-nosed slugs'd be the likely weapon to do that kind of damage in that sequence."

"Or a shotgun up close if it wasn't for the fact that the dining-car windows are sealed shut and it was holed, not shattered."

"What makes you bring it up, then?" Bess asked, setting down a trivet and a brown teapot. There was a sugar bowl already on the table. She brought a jug of milk, some spoons, and one of those plastic lemons full of juice.

"One of the Indian men had a shotgun with him, instead of a rifle. That seems strange to me. I mean young fellas go carrying guns in their cars for a little varmint hunting, a little plinking, it's usually rifles like the rest of them had. I wonder why the one called Abe was toting a shotgun."

"Why do you think?" George asked.

"Because he'd then be the only one who could say for sure that his shot wasn't the one that killed Chaney."

"Isn't that an interesting thought," George said.

Bess sat down and poured for all of us as I went on telling about the talk I'd had with the Indians.

"I've been thinking about some of what they said that bothers me. They all agreed they were maybe farther, but no closer, than a quarter of a mile from the train. About four hundred yards. But one of them said he could see one of the passengers lift his glass like he was toasting him."

"Could you see a thing like that a quarter of a mile away?"

"That's what I'm wondering."

"If you can't, what do you think it means?"

"It means they were a hell of a lot closer or it means somebody else saw it and mentioned it to them."

"Somebody who was closer."

"Somebody who fired the shot that killed Chaney."

Bess had put milk in George's tea and lemon in her own and now she asked me what I wanted.

"Lemon and sugar," I said.

"What else?" George asked, working over the facts and wanting more.

I told him how cool Florence Chaney seemed to take it, yet how she'd gone out of her way to examine her husband's hand—held it—to make sure it was him that'd been killed.

I told them everything I knew about personal relationships in the family, including Banner's remark about Warden being very friendly with Florence Chaney and her story about the mountain climbing which was to illustrate the fact that if Chaney thought

Banner was dead weight then he would've let him go and be justified doing it.

I also mentioned the take-over in progress and how Lewis Warden had hesitated a bit when I asked if Harold Chaney had been against it.

"Who else was along on the climbing expedition?" Bess suddenly asked.

"I don't get your reason for asking, Bess," I said.

"I don't know myself, except it might tell us something about Florence Chaney. Was she off with a party of strangers, like one of those Outward Bound adventures, or was she with relatives? Or was she with a friend, a special friend? Also . . ."

"Yes?"

"I think you'd better have a talk with the stepdaughter."

"And why's that?"

"Because if her stepmother was having an affair with anybody on the side, she'd probably know about it."

Eighteen

THE MINUTE BESS ASKED those two questions, I caught her drift. Here I was thinking about the money involved as being a legitimate reason for suspicion of murder, and there she was thinking about infidelity, jealousy, and other such generators of murderous passion.

"When's the last day Chaney's going to be laid out?" George asked.

"Tomorrow evening they'll be cremating him."

"That gives you time, then. You catch the ten twenty-five out of McCook, it'll get you into Chicago three-thirty tomorrow afternoon. Plenty of time for you to go over to the funeral parlor and question the daughter. Question anybody else she might lead you to as well. They'll probably all be there for the last good-bye."

"I wonder if I could manage a visit to Maggie Wister this evening?" I said.

Bess smiled and George grinned.

"Here we thought you made a special trip just to visit with us," he said.

"I surely came to talk this shooting over with you," I said, "and, as usual, I got corroboration on the technicals from you, George, and inspiration on the intangibles from you, Bess, but there's this other problem that's bothering me, too, and I'd like to see Maggie just to see if I can nail it down."

"Nothing we can help you with?" Bess said.

"Well, I'm sure you'd have some words of wisdom concerning it, but since you've been married—what is it—"

"Thirty-five years," Bess provided.

"Thirty-five years," I repeated. "Since you've been married that long I think maybe it'd be best to take my survey among single women who've been on their own for some time."

Bess threw a little glance at George which told me they'd been talking about my unmarried state lately and that she was taking this so-called survey of mine as evidence that I was about to give in.

"You can use my station wagon," Bess said. "It's been lying there unused through the winter . . ."

"But I turned it over every other day, so it shouldn't give you any trouble," George said, finishing her sentence the way married people will do for one another.

"Stay for supper before you go calling?" Bess asked.

"I think I'd better get over there in daylight," I said. "I'll leave your wagon in front of your office, if that's all right, George."

"You forgot they took Akron off the schedule."

"You forgot I work for the railroad," I replied. "I'll just call in dispatch and tell them I'm asking for a flag stop."

"That should give you an extra thirty minutes with the widow," Bess said.

I made the call to the dispatcher, who promised me he'd get right on to the train and tell them about the unscheduled stop. Then I got the keys to the wagon, shook George's hand, hugged Bess very gently, and went out to start the car.

It started on the second try and I was off to Maggie Wister's little cottage, which was only about three miles outside of town.

It was still plenty light enough when I got there.

I parked the car in the drive and walked up to the door, ready to press the bell which would flash lights in every room in the house. But the door opened up and there she was standing in the open doorway, smiling at me, with a little terrier in her arms.

Maggie's maybe the most sensible woman I know, even including Bess McGilvray. She doesn't confuse issues or try to compare cheese and chalk. The loving friendship we have is one thing, domestic commitment another. I leaned toward her to give her a kiss and that little mutt took a nip at my nose. I almost fell over backward trying to get away from his teeth. Maggie laughed, which I didn't think too polite of her, then quickly covered her mouth with her hand, her eyes filled with contrition.

She nuzzled her face in the dog's neck, making sounds that calmed it down. Then she put it down on the floor at her feet and kissed me properly.

On the way to the parlor she signed that the dog's name was Tippie and he was a Hearing Ear dog, trained to alert her whenever he detected an unusual sound or the approach of a visitor. I looked down at the little wonder dog trotting at our feet, and he looked right back as if to say it was okay with him if I stayed but I better damn well know who was top dog around the house.

Maggie made supper for the two of us, after she fed Tippie, and then I went into the parlor and made a fire in the fireplace before sitting down on the love seat, ready for a cuddle and a chat. Maggie came in with two hot chocolates laced with a smidge of Kahlua, handed me one, and took the other with her over to the wing-back chair, where she curled up with her feet under her.

So, though we hadn't said anything about it at the supper table, it didn't take a detective to see that things had changed in subtle ways in our relationship.

"Can you hear me from over there?" I asked.

She smiled and nodded, letting me know that she could read my lips perfectly well in the light of the floor lamp.

The firelight and the lamp by her chair softly illuminated her face as well, and I had this funny pang shoot through me as though I'd suddenly realized I should have been living the picture I was looking at for twenty years or more.

Her eyebrow went up and she cocked her head a little as though reading my mind, as though saying it wasn't ever too late.

She let go her mug of chocolate with one hand and signed to me, "What's troubling you, Jake?"

"Growing old," I said.

She shook her head a little. I didn't know if she meant I wasn't growing old or if fretting over the inevitable was nothing but foolishness. She passed her hand over her cheeks and signed, "Me, too."

"Not you, Maggie. You never seem to grow a day older from one visit to the next. Maybe it's because you take things so calm. I never saw anyone took things so calm."

She smiled, shook her head again, and turned it to stare into the fire. And I saw, more clearly than I'd ever seen before, just how much it cost her to be alone. To be alone and to be in everlasting silence, too.

I didn't want to have another conversation about

AIDS and the risks of making love and the plague years. Tragic as that was, and as overwhelming as the changes would have to be before cures were found or the plague wore itself out for a while, there were more fundamental things being tested here. The same things that've been tried and tested through the centuries. The whole idea of family and companionship.

Somewhere or other, in a book, in a television show, I remembered reading or hearing that a man needed two things to make a complete life: his work and a comrade. I had my work, but I was beginning to see I had too many comrades and therefore maybe I didn't have any.

All the while I was thinking this, staring into the fire, glancing at Maggie, sipping my hot chocolate, she was looking at me, reading my mind, carrying on a conversation, matching me thought for thought, and never saying a word.

Then Tippie jumped up next to me and put his head on my leg. When Maggie put her mug aside and came over to tuck herself under my arm on the other side, it just about did me in.

Nineteen

When I arrived at the Adams-Winterfield Funeral Home the next afternoon—the last afternoon of the laying out, the afternoon of the brief memorial—it was pretty clear that Florence Chaney's intention of limiting the mourners to just family and a few very close friends had been knocked off the rails.

There was a crowd outside on the lawn and walkways, at least two mobile television units were taping the scene, and I could identify members of the press milling around looking for somebody to interview.

I felt a tap on my shoulder and turned around to see Karen Olliphant, the television reporter, smiling at me like the cat that ate the bird.

"What's this all about, Karen?" I asked.

"I might ask the same question of you, Jake, but I won't. Seeing you here gives me the notion that I won't be wasting my time on a financial obit after all."

"How's that?"

"Where you show up, murder and mayhem are sure to be involved," she said.

"Now, Karen, you met me once during the investigation of a homicide, but that's no reason to assume that murder's my only interest. I'm just a plain old railroad detective usually concerned with nothing more than freight theft and passenger fraud."

"That may be, but murder's the only interest that'd bring you over here to the funeral. You don't seem the sort of man who goes trotting around to such things just for the sociability of it."

"Well, now, you don't know that. I had an aunt once used to check the obituaries. She'd go to view every body that had a name that belonged in the family, by marriage or otherwise. Spent half her life crying into her sleeve for people she didn't even know, on the off chance she might be doing some good for a relative. I might be of the same persuasion."

She tucked her hand through my arm and hugged me to her, dragging me along to get away from the congestion. I enjoyed the contact, so I didn't pull away.

"While we're on the subject," I said, "what brings you here? What you said about me goes for you too. Your beat's not the financial beat, is it?"

"I got sent out on this because it's a little hotter than a simple merger or a take-over postponed because of sudden death. A lawyer for Whente Corporation came out with a public statement this afternoon claiming it was Harold Chaney's intention to sign the papers assigning his shares to them. They already have a signed letter of intent and they're saying that, in Chaney's sudden absence, that stands as a legal agreement. Lewis Warden, as acting CEO, and Florence Chaney, as Chairman of the Board, pro tem, says otherwise."

"Run that train through the station one more time, will you?" I said.

"What's your confusion?"

"Are you telling me that Harold Chaney was welcoming the take-over with open arms and it was the wife and partner who didn't want it?"

"That's the way it looks. It also looks like it's boiling up into a fight between Whente and Florence Chaney, now that Harold's gone and she has the voting power of his shares."

"Nobody knows that for sure, do they?"

"What do you mean?"

"Nobody knows that Chaney left those shares to his wife, do they? The will hasn't been probated or even read, has it?"

"I just assumed," Karen said.

"That a man'd leave something like that to his wife?"

"Well, yes."

"He had plenty of other things. With or without the shares, I'm sure Florence Chaney's still a wealthy woman."

Karen looked thoughtful.

"Well," she finally said, "it's something to think about, though I can't figure out what it means right this minute."

"You'll have to excuse me," I said, disengaging her hand from my sleeve. "I've got some things to do inside."

She wouldn't stay disengaged but grabbed onto my arm with both hands, smiled sweetly, and said, "You'll look a lot less conspicuous with a wife on your arm, Jake."

"Wife? Well, for Lord's sake, you're young enough to be my daughter."

"That's true," she said, moving me along and

matching me stride for stride, her hip riding along with mine like a matched pair of high-steppers, "but twenty years' difference never counted for much between a man and a woman. In fact, there are some working it the other way around. Older women marrying younger men."

She'd worked us through the crowd outside the front door right up onto the porch, then backed off half a step to let me take the lead. I was stopped at the door by a young man in gray pants and a maroon sports jacket with a black and gold coat of arms embroidered on the pocket and a permanent band of black satin sewn around the right sleeve.

"Family and invited guests only," he whispered. "I'm sorry."

"Has the service started?" I whispered back.

"Not for another fifteen minutes," he murmured.

"This lady has to use the facility downstairs, next to the smoking room," I murmured back, showing him that I was familiar with the layout of his establishment. "She's pregnant and in some distress."

The youngster's eyes went to Karen's middle, but her coat didn't let him see much. He dithered a minute, then stepped aside and let us go through, me holding onto her elbow like she was fragile and Karen trying to keep from busting out laughing.

The crowd was thinner inside.

I put my ear up close to Karen's. Her hair smelled sweet.

"Maybe it's not such a bad idea you go downstairs and sit in the lounge."

"No, you don't," she said. "Where you go, I go."

"I'm going to try and talk to Harold Chaney's daughter. I can't do it inside while the service is about to start. I'm going to get her out of there and downstairs where it's quieter if I can."

"Don't try to trick me, Jake. I can help you question her. The woman's touch, you know."

"Hush. Go do like I ask you to do."

She surprised me by turning away and going to the stairs, which was just as well because the kid with the mourning band on his sleeve was keeping an eye on us.

I went up to the open doors of the slumber room where another Adams-Winterfield employee stood guard. I didn't say a word, just flipped my badge at him and pantomimed that I was just going to stand in the back and make myself invisible.

He wanted to take it farther but he didn't. Whenever you're around funeral homes you can work on the assumption that the closer you get to the coffin the less likely the undertakers will do anything that might make a scene.

I stood in the back for about a minute or two, getting the lay of things.

Not every seat was taken, so I judged I was well ahead of time for the memorial ceremony. There was an aisle on each side and one in the center. The stage where the coffin with the photograph on its lid stood took up half of the front of the room. A small grouping of chairs off to the right was for the use of the family.

Sometimes the family is secluded in privacy behind a screen, but Florence Chaney, or whoever else made the decision, had done away with that and they were all out there for everyone to see.

I saw the old lady and her nurse-companion, Maddy, sitting side by side, their chairs moved away far enough to separate them from the others spiritually if not physically.

Just across the space sat Chaney's daughter, close enough to reach out and take her grandmother's hand, which she did just that minute. Florence Chaney was sitting next to her stepdaughter, with the stepson on the other side.

Milton Banner and Lewis Warden sat in the second row with one other person and an empty seat. The three chairs in the third row were filled with people I didn't know.

I felt somebody's eyes on me. When I looked I saw Marcus Sears looking at me. He was sitting on the center aisle, dressed for the funeral in a black coat, gray vest, and black tie. His hands were resting on his walking stick, holding on to a pair of gray gloves and a black homburg. All of a sudden he didn't look like a financial mover and shaker but like a bit player in a drawing-room comedy, waiting for the curtain to fall so he could go home and soak his feet. He raised an eyebrow at me, asking me what I was doing there, and I turned my eyes to the family group then back to him.

He raised his left hand a little and I shook my head, telling him that I wasn't interested in the old lady and her nurse who sat apart. He held up one finger and I nodded. The person I wanted to speak to was in the first row. He raised his left hand slightly again, signing that he'd start counting from the left. I nodded right away on one. He got up, turned and placed his hat and gloves on the chair, and went over to the family group.

I could tell he'd already presented himself once and delivered his condolences. Both Florence Chaney and Lewis Warden leaned forward as though they thought he wanted to speak to one of them, but he smiled them away and leaned in close to whisper to the bereaved daughter. She looked a little uncertain about what he was saying, but it was clear she was brought up to respect important elders and followed him up the aisle without more than a second's hesitation.

I backed out of the slumber room, but before I went across the reception hall and down the stairs, I asked the undertaker's assistant how I'd know when the memorial was about to start.

"If you're going downstairs for a smoke you'll hear three organ chords," he said.

Just like dimming the lights at the theater, I thought before I went on along down to the lounge.

Karen was the only one sitting in the smoking room but she wasn't smoking. She stood up when Sears and the girl walked in.

"Jessica, this is Mr. Jake Hatch," Sears said. "Mr. Hatch, this is Jessica Chaney, Harold's daughter."

According to what I'd been told, Jessica would have to be twenty-one or twenty-two, but she had the fragile look and the manner of a girl of fifteen or sixteen. I could see she was very puzzled about why Sears had plucked her out of the slumber room and marched her down the aisle for everybody to see, down here to be confronted by a rumpled-looking man and a competent-looking young woman.

I introduced Karen around and a little frown appeared between my friend Sears's eyebrows.

"Don't I know you, Miss Olliphant? You look familiar. Of course. I've seen you on the television news at times when business has taken me to Denver." He turned his frown to me. "I don't know, Jake."

"Karen and me got a deal, Marcus. We help each other out and we respect the confidence of whatever one tells the other isn't for publication."

"All right then."

"Will you tell me what's going on, Mr. Sears?" Jessica said in a soft, childish voice, which had little bits of iron filings buried in it.

For all her passive ways and under-the-lashes glances, soft voice, and small gloved hands, Jessica wasn't a young woman without spirit or resources.

"Mr. Hatch is a detective for the Burlington Northern Railroad."

"Oh yes, Florence mentioned you to us."

"That's good," I said. "Everything's very straightforward here. I want you to know that. Will you sit down for a minute?"

"The ceremony's going to start soon," she said.

"Not for a little while yet. We've got time. Please, sit down and let me ask you a few questions. It won't take very long."

Sears touched her elbow, and that was enough to make her defer to him and do as I'd asked her to do. She sat down facing the door to the hall. I sat down next to her. Sears took a seat a few chairs away like he didn't want to eavesdrop on a private conversation, though he could probably hear perfectly well as long as we didn't lean close and whisper.

She wouldn't let him get away with it. She turned to him and in a low voice said, "What is your interest in arranging this interview between us, Mr. Sears?"

"You know and understand my position at the Board of Trade?"

"Of course."

"Then you must know that since your father's death there's some confusion about what his position had been concerning the impending take-over of Chaney Enterprises by the Whente Corporation. Anything that upsets the calm and open conduct of business is of some concern to me."

"Yes, I understand."

She removed her gloves as she glanced up at Karen, who was still standing. Karen sat down in a chair across the room, next to the doorway that led out into a hall that served the rest rooms too.

Jessica's hands were small and well-shaped. She spent a lot of time working with them, because they were brown and strong, the right hand smudged with ingrained dirt around the crotch of the thumb. Not the kind of hands for fancy rings.

She looked at me with gray eyes that had those same little iron filings in them. "I have no idea how I can enlighten you on that matter any more than a half a dozen others might do."

"I understand that. But we've been getting conflicting reports on how your father felt about the take-over. Most say he was ready to fight it. A couple say he welcomed it. I thought he might've talked to you or your brother, since it was your future he was dealing with as much as his."

"My father wasn't the sort to discuss his plans—even the plans he had for others—with anyone, least of all the people who would be most affected by his decisions."

"Why do you think that was?"

She looked at me as though she didn't think I was very bright.

"Because my father saw himself as the patriarch."

"Not a stern man? Not strict or mean?"

She waved her stained right hand in front of her face. "No, no. Permissive. Indulgent. In anything but the management of finances. In that area he not only believed that he knew best, he believed that he was the only one that knew anything at all."

"So he would've just gone ahead and arranged secure financial futures for his mother, his wife, and his children without discussion or consultation?"

"That's correct."

"And he didn't discuss the take-over with you or your brother?"

"Never directly with me. You might ask Mark if he spoke to him about it, but I doubt it, since Mark would have mentioned it to me. But for what it may be worth to you"—she turned her head to look at Marcus Sears again—"I had the impression that my father welcomed the offer."

"Why do you think that was? He was still pretty young for retirement—a dynamo like your father."

"He wanted a new life," she said, suddenly looking at me with a frankness that told me she'd made up her mind about something while we'd been talking and was ready to tell me the truth about anything I wanted to ask. But I also could see this strong loyalty to family and the tradition of confidentiality that people with money seem to develop more than most. Whatever I was going to get I was going to have to dig for, she wasn't going to dump it in my lap.

I knew how to play that game. It was like fly fishing. You just kept on pulling the lure back and dapping it out again, choosing a different spot each time, until all of a sudden the fish came leaping up out of the shadows and took the bait. Then you could just reel it in.

I thought of Bess's two questions.

"You remember when your stepmother went on the mountain-climbing expedition?"

"I went along with her," Jessica said.

"Just you and her?"

"Oh no, there was a party of people. There were twelve of us in all, plus two guides."

"I meant were you and your stepmother strangers to the rest of the group, or did friends go along?"

"My Uncle Milton went along, but he refused to climb. Not even the lower slopes. He just stayed in the lodge and drank and made sketches of the cloud formations."

"I didn't know that your uncle and your stepmother were that friendly."

"How friendly do you mean?"

"Friendly enough to spend that much time together in a small group of people on the edge of nowhere."

"My father treated him to the vacation. He thought it would do Uncle Milton some good."

"So your father decided things for people besides financial matters?"

"Occasionally. Milton was a special case. Nobody knows what to do about Uncle Milton. I don't know what was in my father's mind, sending him off to climb mountains. I don't know what he expected to happen."

"Was there anyone else you knew on the expedition?"

"Mr. Pickering and his wife."

"Terrence Pickering?"

"That's right," she said, looking at me in some surprise, as though it would be pretty remarkable for anyone to know so many Pickerings that they'd have to be identified by first names.

"I thought he was a business rival of your father's."

"Florence and Sheila Pickering, Terry's wife, were friends."

"Good friends?"

"No, just social." She smiled briefly. "We're all very civilized. We don't let differences in one arena interfere with intercourse in another."

I didn't know if the smile was a little sardonic—if she was enjoying a private joke and speaking with double meanings—or if she was giving me a clue.

"Mrs. Chaney says she never made the climb for the summit," I went on.

"No. It was decided she didn't have the strength for it."

"Did you make the climb?"

"Yes."

"But not your Uncle Milton."

"That's right."

"Anybody else not make the climb?"

She hesitated a second.

"Mr. Pickering turned his ankle on the lower slopes and decided against it."

There was a flush on Jessica's cheeks and neck, as though she was excited by hinting to a stranger that her stepmother had perhaps had a little go-round with a man her father didn't like.

"Do you remember if one or more of the guides or porters may have been North American Indians?"

"I didn't have much conversation with the men hired to take us on the climb."

It'd just been a long cast.

Someone came tapping along the tiled corridor. A woman passed by wearing a mink coat with the collar up and a hat to match. She was crying and had a handkerchief up to her mouth, so all I could see was part of a face and a flash of red hair.

She sensed our eyes on her and paused for a beat, looking into the room with a sweeping glance and then fixing on Jessica.

I looked at the girl. Her hands were still, balled up in little fists. The splinters of iron in her eyes had turned to knives.

The woman gasped and hurried on.

"Who's that?" I asked, quick and sharp.

"I don't know," Jessica stammered. "I thought it was someone who used to work for my father a long time ago."

"Who would that be?"

"Marla Kassabian." She collected herself. "But that wasn't her."

Then the first chord of the organ warned us that the memorial was about to begin.

Twenty

After that first organ chord, Jessica stood up without a word and went upstairs with Marcus Sears, trying to catch up so it could be seen he was escorting her back.

At the door he paused long enough to tell me with a gesture of his hand that he wanted to know anything I might find out about the crying woman, having read about as much from her response to Jessica's look of hate as I'd done.

Karen's eyes had been elsewhere or something, because, though she knew something had happened, she didn't know what.

"You learn anything, Jake?" she asked.

"You see Jessica's hands?"

"What about them?"

"You tell me."

"They were smudged with soot or something."

"All around the curve of her thumb and forefinger?"

"That's right."

"Gunpowder. I didn't have to ask, but if I did ask was she a marksman you can bet she'd say she was. It takes a lot of shooting to stain somebody's hand that way."

"You're not saying she shot her father?"

"I'm just saying there's a hell of a lot of people fooling around with guns and rifles in this situation."

"Do you think this Terrence Pickering is going to turn out to be a rifleman too?"

"Without a doubt."

The second chord sounded.

"She was telling us what I think she was telling us, wasn't she?" Karen said.

"What's that?"

"That Florence Chaney and Terrence Pickering were doing a number up there in the lodge while the others climbed the mountain?"

"I'd say so. But we don't want to forget that Uncle Milton was there."

"That might've been why Harold Chaney sent him along on the expedition. To keep an eye out."

"I'd say that's a possibility. Though, if I wanted a watchdog to look after my straying wife, Milton Banner'd be the last one I'd choose."

The third chord slipped through the funeral home.

"Are we waiting for something?" Karen asked.

"I'm waiting for that woman to come back out of the ladies' room. Go have a look, will you?"

Karen went to have a look and came right back out shaking her head. There was an exit door to the parking lot at the end of the corridor.

I went to it and tried the knob. It was unlocked.

"Let's go get a cup of coffee and talk," I said.

We found a shop about a block and a half away. Karen ordered tea and I ordered coffee with a sweet roll.

"That's no kind of a lunch," Karen said.

"It's not lunch."

"Well, then you shouldn't be eating between meals. Who do you suppose that woman was?"

"Harold Chaney's mistress."

"My God, you take long steps," Karen said, leaning back in the booth with her mouth open in exaggerated surprise.

"A woman comes to a funeral advertised as being for family and close friends. Luckily there's a crowd, so maybe she figures she can get lost and sit in the room and pay her last respects to the man she loved. But it gets to be too much for her. She wants to cry and can't do it publicly. So she comes downstairs and is seen by the man's daughter, who pretty clearly recognizes her. She takes off through the side door and goes home to mourn by herself."

"Why did Jessica say she knew her and then change her mind?"

"She answered me because she was startled at seeing her come walking past the doorway. Then she tried to take it back. She'd already busted the code by telling us about her stepmother's little affair. You expect her to open up her father's secret life, too, and make the family out to be a bunch of alley cats?"

"It always gets back to that, doesn't it?"

"What's it always get back to?"

"Sex and money. Money and sex."

Twenty-one

ALL OF A SUDDEN I had more possibilities to look into than I really wanted. But there was only one thing I felt I had to do and that was have another talk with the Indian kids.

Nobody had to tell me why they'd moved them to Marshalltown from Indianola. They weren't worried about them breaking out, they were worried about somebody breaking in.

By and large the people of Iowa and Nebraska are about the least prejudiced people I ever met, but when times are hard and jobs scarce you can always find some malcontents ready to blame it on "the kikes, the niggers, the redskins" or whoever's handy, and beat them up to show how manly they are.

After the state attorney decided to bring heavy charges against the Indians, there might be reason to fear some rabble-rouser would work a bunch of beered-up men into a mob one night and maybe go over to whatever jail the accused were locked up in and drag them out for a beating.

Two things made Marshalltown a better place to incarcerate them. It was a bigger, better-manned jail, and it was close to the Mesquakie Indian Settlement where they could be sheltered if it looked like what could happen happened.

I took the train to Osceola and then drove a company car the fifty-two miles to Des Moines and another fifty-one to Marshalltown, getting there close to half an hour after midnight.

Identification or no identification, credentials or no credentials, Al Bunty, the man in charge, wasn't about to let me in to see the Indians.

"If you ask them, I'd bet they'll want to talk to me."

"Be that as it may," he said, not even bothering to get up from behind his desk. "They could say yes now, and later on they could say their civil rights was abused."

"How's that?"

"Waking them up after lights out. They could claim their sleep was disturbed."

I made a whoosh which meant he was really reaching for it.

He cocked an eye at me. "Say what you want, things funnier than that happen nowadays."

"I only need to speak to one of them. Maybe you could take a look and see if one of them was still awake."

"I could tell you stories," he said, as though he hadn't even heard me.

I was ready to listen to any stories he had to tell, but right then a couple of uniformed officers came in with two drunks in tow and started the booking process. I figured Bunty didn't want any more of me.

"What time in the morning?" I asked.

"I'll do you the favor. Ten o'clock. Visiting's not usual till afternoon."

"Ten o'clock," I said, and started to walk off.

"Hey!" he said, and I stopped.

He came out from behind his desk and walked me over toward the door a few steps, out of earshot of the two uniforms and the drunks.

"Hey, the railroads ever give out passes anymore?"

"There are times when we can write a complimentary pass."

"Good for what?"

"One round trip anywhere along the line."

"Anywhere along Amtrak coast to coast?"

"Well, no, anywhere along the Burlington Northern tracks."

"Which is what?"

"Which is from coast to coast except for California, New York, or New England."

"Would I have to drive to Osceola?" he asked.

"What for? You'd do better going to Ottumwa."

"You mean if I was going to Chicago?"

"Well, if you were going anywhere. I mean it'd be a shorter automobile drive to Ottumwa than to Osceola."

Here it was after midnight, one drunk throwing up all over himself, another one laughing, two cops cursing, and I was trying to help a jailer figure out if it was worth doing me a favor for a round trip on the railroad.

"Can you make that two passes?"

"One for the wife?" I said, and took out my wallet, where I keep a couple of trip authorization blanks.

"So, you'll go have a look and see if any one of those Indian men wants to talk to me?"

"If any of them are awake. There's only four of them, you know?"

"Oh?"

"Two are over at the juvenile facility in Cedar Rapids."

"Okay. I'll write out these passes while you're having a look."

He went off toward the door to the cells.

"You want me to have this sucker clean that up?" one of the cops said as he passed.

"I'll get the trusty to do it. I don't want to have to go looking for a mop and a pail right now."

I went back to his desk and wrote out the passes.

The uniforms put the drunks into the holding cell.

In a few minutes Bunty was back.

"The one called Abe is still awake. He says he'll see you. I can't go opening up the visiting room this time of night. You'll have to talk to him with him in the cell and you outside."

"If that's as comfortable as it's going to get, it's all right with me," I said.

"I'm going to have to pat you down," he said.

I stood up and held my arms out to my sides. "Go to it."

He did a quick and thorough job of it. Then he walked me over to the door to the cells and let me through.

"Halfway down on the left," he said. "Make it five minutes."

I nodded and walked on through. The corridor with the cells on both sides smelled heavily of disinfectant, but it couldn't mask the odor of so many sleeping, half-washed men. Somebody grumbled in his sleep.

Abe was standing at the bars dressed in just a pair of jeans. His feet and upper body were bare. He was clutching the bars. He looked like a deer caged up. I know if there was a way for me to open that door, he'd start to run and maybe even try to run through the wall.

"Who's in there with you?" I asked.

"Dan Pool."

"Which ones were the young ones?"

"Willy and Charlie. They're over to Grand Rapids."

"I know."

"They're going to try them separately."

"Same charges?"

"Malicious mischief and the unlawful discharge of a weapon."

"How about you?"

"Manslaughter, aggravated assault . . ."

He took his hands off the bars and spread them out for a moment, saying he didn't know what else they were being charged with but there was more.

"So that means Calgary and . . ."

"Rider," he said, filling it in for me.

". . . are next door?"

"That's right."

"What's your full name, Abe?"

"Loping Wolf."

"I mean . . ."

"Anglo name?"

"How they booked you."

"Abraham Woodman. What do you want to know for?"

"I don't know," I said, shrugging my shoulders.

"Well, it's polite of you to ask."

He was pretty sick of being called by his first name on first meeting, the way people talk to children.

"Can I still call you Abe?"

"Can I call you Jake?"

We both grinned.

"I'd hope so," I said.

"Is there anything you can do for us?" he said.

"I was just about to ask you the same question."

"I told you what happened, the way it happened.

We got a little beered up and went looking for things to plink. We just happened to meet that goddamn train and acted damn foolish."

"No, no. I don't think it was a random bullet from one of your rifles that killed Harold Chaney."

"I'm glad to hear you say that."

"I think it was a deliberate killing shot fired from a rifle with a scope by a marksman probably lying prone and resting the muzzle on a tripod or a ridge on the ground."

"Well, that's good news," he said. "We were in pickups. Everybody on the train saw that."

"That's right. But you know there's two things that bother me about that story?"

"What's that?"

"One is that you say you were no closer than a quarter of a mile and maybe as far as half a mile when you were running parallel to the train, but Willy said one of the people in the dining car raised a glass of wine to him."

"Willy's only a kid. He sees things he wants to see. He was probably trying to give you the idea of how friendly it all seemed at the time."

"Or he could be repeating something he heard from another mouth. The other thing is, if there was this shooter lying in a fold of the land as the train went by, how handy it'd be if six Indians in two trucks went by at the same time, taking shots at the trains like a bunch of redskins out of the Wild West."

"That's a lot of speculation," he said.

"Now, there's a fine word, a fine, educated word."

"I'm not illiterate, Jake."

"I never thought you were. I think you put it on and take it off according to how it pleases you."

"What's that?"

"Your Indian blanket. Who were you visiting at the Settlement?"

"I'm not visiting. I belong there. I run the bingo hall."

"Bingo's a concession run by outsiders. I know that."

"I didn't say I ran the game, I said I managed the hall. That belongs to us—to the Indians—we only lease it out for this and that. Concerts, club meetings, dances, and the bingo games. They only come in two nights a week, you know? I have to make the hall pay a profit the rest of the week too."

"Your representative from the Bureau of Indian Affairs been consulting with you on this?"

He looked at a spot somewhere over my right shoulder.

"Oh, I get it," I said. "You've been letting everybody believe you were all reservation Indians under the protection and supervision of the Bureau, but you're not."

"What are you talking about? Ain't you heard? Us redskins can come and go as we please."

"I know that. But you and I both know an Indian living on the reservation can expect more consideration from the Bureau than one that's living out in the world. So, are any of you living inside Mesquakie?"

"No. Calgary and Rider have a place to sleep in Tama. Willy and Charlie live with their folks in Toledo."

"How about you and Dan Pool?"

He hesitated.

"Where do you live?"

"Dan Pool lives with a woman in Montezuma."

"That's south. How about you?"

"I live further south in New Sharon."

"Getting closer to Ottumwa, ain't we? Live on your own?"

"All on my own."

"You got a lawyer?"

"Sure."

"From the Bureau or local public defenders?"

"Juvenile Authority's got their own lawyers looking out for Willy and Charlie. Calgary and Rider have a lawyer from the Bureau."

"How about you and Dan Pool?"

"He's got his and I've got mine."

"Defenders?"

"Private."

"You mind telling me their names?"

"What for?"

"It's a matter of public record. I just want to save myself the extra effort."

"I don't know the name of Dan Pool's lawyer. Mine's name is Jack Hedrick."

"Where's his office?"

"Chicago."

"Oh?"

"Don't the best lawyers always work out of the big cities?"

"I don't know about that, but I reckon the most expensive lawyers do. One other thing. How come you were the only one with a shotgun?"

"I had it with me because I'd had some complaints about rats in the bingo hall. I've been sitting outside watching for them and blowing them away. Shotgun does a surer job than a rifle. Those little bastards are quick."

I told Abe I'd be seeing him, maybe, and walked off down the corridor. I paused for a beat along the way long enough to make sure the grumble I heard was coming from Abe's cell. Dan Pool had been awake through it all. He was giving Abe hell until Abe said something in Indian which I expect was similar to a commonly used American word.

Out at the charge desk I asked the sergeant if I could use the phone with my credit card.

I knew that Marcus Sears stayed up half the night. We'd had a long talk about how old folks started sleeping less and less as though trying to crowd in more living before it was over.

I didn't argue with him, although I find that I've been wanting to sleep more and more. Marcus Sears would laugh at that and say it was because I was still a pup.

He picked up on the second ring.

"At your desk, Marcus?" I said.

"In my study and at my desk, Jake."

"Working?"

"Reading *Bleak House.*"

"Coincidence?"

"About what?"

"My question's about a lawyer."

"Which lawyer would that be?"

"Jack Hedrick."

"I know of him."

"Good man?"

"I've never heard otherwise."

"Have you heard about him lately?"

"I've seen his name on a document of some sort."

"Remember where?"

There was a considerable pause and then he said, "No, I'm afraid not, Jake."

"Maybe on a document having to do with Chaney Enterprises?"

"Give me a minute."

I could tell he'd tucked the phone between his shoulder and jaw, got up from the desk, and was going through files.

"In this age of the copying machine, I keep duplicates of practically everything here at my home," he said. "Here they are. Papers about the Whente stock offer. Chaney Enterprises' initial response on the company letterhead. Jack Hedrick. Half a dozen legal firms. Here it is. Malcolm, Seagrave, Morrison, and

Hedrick. Also Jack Hedrick on the board of directors. That's something."

"What do you mean?"

"Hedrick's firm is a full-service legal conglomerate but Jack Hedrick, himself, specializes in tort law."

"Personal injury?"

"Among other things."

"That can involve criminal actions as well, can't it?"

"It can. What have you got, Jake?"

"Nothing but suspicions."

"You going to tell me any of them?"

"For one thing, I'm wondering how come a young Indian, manages a bingo hall at Mesquakie, hires a Chicago lawyer to defend him against a charge of manslaughter."

"The answer probably is that someone hired the lawyer for him. Is that all I can do for you, Jake?"

"That's all. By the way, the first time I asked you to fill me in about Chaney, you never mentioned that you were such a close friend of the family."

He chuckled. It came over the phone like he was standing right in the room grinning and twinkling his eyes at me. "I wasn't trying to hide it, Jake. It just wasn't part of the information package you asked for."

Twenty-two

IOWA HASN'T GOT MUCH by way of Indian reservations, the Mesquakie Settlement being the only one.

Nebraska's got Winnebago, a big reservation about twenty miles south of Sioux City, and another, for the Santee Sioux, up on the South Dakota border.

If memory serves, there was an office of the Bureau of Indian Affairs in Omaha, but I'd make no bets on it.

I asked Al Bunty if he happened to know.

"You're looking for an Indian agent?" he said.

"I'd like to find out what they're going to do about those boys in there, if anything."

"They're already doing. A fella by the name of Simms Beecher arrived yesterday—day before yesterday—afternoon and had a talk with them. Offered them the services of legal counsel and so forth."

Of course. Abe told me that. But I didn't think it through, maybe taking it for granted that it was all arranged over the phone the way most things are nowadays. Or maybe I was just getting tired. Or old. Or careless.

"You hear what I said?" Bunty asked.

"I think I'm getting punchy. I've been riding trains and driving cars half the day. That agency fella still in town?"

"I guess. He said he'd be back again to have another talk with my prisoners."

"I'd like to have a talk with him," I said.

"What's your hurry? If it's about them Indians, they ain't going anywhere. If I was you, I'd just go across the street to the hotel and get me some sleep. Start fresh in the morning."

I said I thought that was a very good idea.

The hotel wasn't much but it had a restaurant and a bar, which I figured was the only bar downtown still open. Hotel bars are like that, serving all the night-birds and wakeful travelers who search for some small comfort while on the road.

While I was checking in, a burst of laughter came out through the barroom doors into the lobby, which decided me on having a short toddy to soothe me a little.

The saloon was all wood and brass and low-level lighting, more like an English pub than an American cocktail lounge. There were only five people in the place, including the bartender, a small group to be making so much noise.

There was a woman, about forty-five years old, wearing a summer-weight print dress. She was perched on the bar stool with her legs crossed so that her skirt rode up her thighs. I figured she was the local lady of favors, a fixture like the hat rack at the entrance, where a quarter of a dozen overcoats and a couple of hats were hanging.

I added mine, took a stool at the end, and counted the rest of the noses.

There was one like a beak on a man who looked like an old Western undertaker, big hands and wristbones sticking out of a white shirt a size too small. Smile like a row of tombstones.

He was listening to the fella telling the jokes, a red-faced salesman-type man who knew he was hell with the ladies and everybody's instant pal.

The comedian spotted me and lowered his voice as though he wanted me to lean in closer if I wanted a piece of the fun.

There was another burst of laughter as the bartender walked over to get my order. The undertaker was busy laughing at the joke, checking me out, and looking down the lady's dress, all at the same time.

The fourth member of the pickup party was a neat-looking fella wearing cord trousers and a brown tweed jacket with leather patches at the elbows. He looked at me and sort of winked, as though wanting even a stranger to know he hadn't invited the company he found himself in. I could see he was the quiet type who could fit in everywhere without any effort at all.

"Small rye and branch," I said.

When the barkeep came back with it, I said, "Who's the comedian?"

"Ernie Shipstead. Runs the hardware store. Doesn't open until nine. Lets him live it up half the night."

I was watching the action as we talked. The quiet fella said something. The lady laughed and said, "Oh, Beech, that was a good one."

"Beech?" I said. "He local?"

"No. He's down from Omaha. Something to do about them Indians they got in the jail across the street."

I took out my wallet and handed him one of my cards. "Would you hand this to Mr. Beecher and—"

"Beech. I think his name's Beech."

"Well, yes, that's what I heard the lady call him, but I think it's short for Beecher. Let's see, okay?"

"Suit yourself. It's no secret."

He glanced at it, then looked up at me with some interest.

"I'm here about those young fellas across the street, too," I said. "Ask him if he'll join me over at that corner table. And bring another one of these and whatever he's having, will you?"

I went over to the table, which was another twenty feet away from the bunch at the bar, as the bartender went over to give Beecher my card.

He excused himself to the others and came over right away. The two men and the woman stopped chattering and laughing and looked our way, three crows on a fence. One with pretty fair legs for its age.

Beecher sat down right away and put out his hand. "Mr. Hatch?"

"Make it Jake, will you, Mr. Beecher?"

"Everybody calls me Beech."

"I heard," I said, jerking my chin toward the lady. "That's what gave me the clue to who you were."

Beech looked over at her too. She was looking at him in a wistful way, as though she regretted him leaving her alone with the other two yahoos.

"Is she the hotel comfort blanket?" I asked.

"I guess," he said. "She seems like a nice woman to be ending up with one of those two."

"I think she has hopes she'll be ending up with you."

He shook his head and looked down at the drink between his hands. "I've got a wife and I don't play or stray. How about you?"

"I'm not a married man. Never have been. But I'll tell you, a lot of my lady friends are giving me reasons why I should give up the single life."

"Think you can do it?"

"I don't know. Old dogs and new tricks and all like that. I've been a long time alone and you forget how to live with somebody on a steady basis."

"If you ever knew."

"There's that. So you're from Indian Affairs?"

"I'm the field agent."

"You know them boys over in the jailhouse?"

"Personally? From before this business? Just two of them."

"Which two?"

"Dan Pool and Abraham Woodman. From the Santee Sioux Reservation. They weren't living there, just passing through, eating and sleeping on the arm."

"You know them separate or as a team?"

He cocked an eye at me as the bartender came over, set down the glasses and my tab.

"You already figure out those two run in tandem?" Beecher said.

"What's to figure out? Two of them are nothing but teenagers. The other two are country Indians. That Dan Pool and Abe are city boys. They know their way around."

"Yes, they do."

"Either one of them ever do any hard time?"

"Not that I know of. There's no record of anything heavy against them."

"How about anything light?"

"Lots of arrests, not many trials, no convictions, except on little things like car theft and unarmed robbery when they were about as young as Willy and Charlie."

"They move around much?"

"Plenty. As far west as Los Angeles, as far east as New York. Dan Pool roamed around Mexico and even as far down as Tierra del Fuego on his own a couple of years ago, I've been told."

"Where were those two born?"

"Abraham Woodman's from outside Chicago. Dan Pool from right around here."

"But not in the Settlement?"

He shook his head and took a swallow of his fresh soda.

"You have anything to do with Abe getting the job as manager of the reservation hall they rent out for bingo?" I asked.

He nodded. "Like in the army. It's not fair, but it's the screw-ups who often end up with the plum jobs and the promotions. A man does good and keeps quiet, there's nothing that needs taking care of. A man's a misfit, he also becomes a challenge. First thing you know, he's something that maybe can be fixed. His good record becomes a bureaucrat's accomplishment."

"So you give him a shot at something interesting."

"Or profitable."

"Or with a little prestige."

"And you've got a productive man who doesn't make as many waves."

"So that's Abe."

"No, that's Dan Pool. He's the bad one. But he listens to Woodman for some reason. Where Woodman goes Dan Pool usually goes. So I just added a little twist to the theory. I gave Abe the responsibility and made Dan Pool his assistant."

"Two birds with one stone."

"That was the idea."

"But how come you tossed these plums at outsiders? Indians from off the reservation?"

"Up in the Santee, they were representing themselves as recruiters for some new political movement. The government would rather not. We had enough trouble with Wounded Knee and the American Indian Church and Marlon Brando."

"I recollect," I said. "You much against them agitating for their rights?"

"I'm all for it. I like to know the depth of a man's sincerity though. I like to know is he militating for a cause or for personal profit."

"And you figured Abe Woodman and Dan Pool were into this new movement for personal profit?"

"I didn't say it was part of any deal, but when I got them the management jobs, their recruiting slowed down and then stopped."

"Slowed down first and then stopped? What was the frosting on the cake?"

"They came to me with plans to set up an Olympic-class firing range for all manner of pistols and rifles. I said I'd support it at the highest level I could reach."

"You drum up any support for their scheme?"

"I asked around for private interest first before I approached the Bureau."

"Like where?"

"Rifle Association. Private gun clubs. Competing marksmen with international reputations."

"What kind of luck did you have?"

"I managed to get several interested parties together at the Mesquakie hall one evening about two months ago. Enthusiasts from as far west as Omaha and as far east as Gary. People from Wisconsin and Minnesota too. Seven states all told."

"Anybody from Chicago?"

"Oh yes. Lewis Warden and the Chaneys came."

"Harold Chaney and his wife Florence?"

"His son and daughter too. They're all into something. Skeet or bench shooting."

"So, there's a connection between those Indians and the man who got shot."

"Well, they were acquainted."

"You told the police?"

"I told the state attorney's office."

I sat there quiet for a minute, trying to think that one through. Trying to figure out if that could explain the heavy charges.

Finally I asked him the question I knew we'd both played with. "Do you think either one of them is capable of murdering somebody for pay?"

That question, said out loud, seemed to shake Beecher a little. He let go his glass of ginger ale and put his hands flat on the table. Then he stared at them for a minute.

"I think maybe anybody'd be capable of murder if the price was right."

"Something like how many millions of dollars?"

"Yes, something like that."

"Well, that's a little more hypothetical than I wanted to be. How about for something a lot less than a million, or even fifty thousand? Something reasonable?"

"If there's anything like a reasonable price for murder I'd have to say I don't know if they wouldn't do it. But if I had to pick one of them, I'd have to say that Abraham Woodman would more likely be the one who'd kill for money than Dan Pool."

"Why's that?"

"Dan Pool's got the fire, but Abraham Woodman's got the grit. Pool's got the lack of conscience, but Woodman's got the smarts. What I mean is, Dan Pool would more likely kill offhandedly, but Woodman might murder in cold blood."

Twenty-three

THE MESQUAKIE INDIAN SETTLEMENT was only about seventeen or eighteen miles southeast of Marshalltown. There was no particular reason for me to go down there nosing around, but on the other hand there wasn't a reason in the world why I shouldn't.

Jim Willows, the tribe's elected chief, was a chunky fifty-five-year-old wearing horn-rimmed eyeglasses. He was carrying a paunch on him half again as big as mine. He wore his hair long and knotted up in a bun in back, Navaho style, which I doubt was a Mesquakie custom. He was wearing a regular fedora like mine except I made do with a plain grosgrain band and his was braided horsehair and blue beads with a spray of feathers as big as a man's palm stuck in the right side.

He saw me looking and must've thought I was admiring it, because he said, "The talisman isn't authentic. It's something to sell to the tourists."

"You get many?"

"Outside of the bingo players, you mean?"

"Yeah, except for them."

"We get a few. We run a couple of festivals. We do some dancing. It gives the women something to look forward to. A way for them to make a little extra money. For six days twice a year we play Indian for the white people. It doesn't count for much."

"You farm, don't you?"

"Oh yes, we do that, so that means we get to hurt when times are bad just like our white farm brothers. But we also hurt when times are good because we can't buy and sell farmland the way they do."

"You saying you got no edge?"

"We got no edge except we got an angle."

"Bingo?"

"That's right. We can run bingo in the meeting hall without worrying any about the gaming laws."

"So, that's something."

"It's all we've got."

"How about the firing range?"

"Abraham Woodman's idea?"

"Yes, that one."

"It was looking pretty good. You put together a first-class facility and you can attract national matches, bring in coaches, set up summer programs just like they do with golf and tennis."

"Is Woodman a good shot?"

"I don't know. He's city born and bred. Some of them running around in pickup trucks with rifles in a rack behind their heads do it more for show than for use. Probably shoot themselves in the foot they try to hit anything faster than a tin can. Woodman? I don't know. I've been with him when he took some hip shots at a row of bottles but I didn't particularly notice."

"How about Dan Pool?"

"I saw him fire with a scope from the prone position at a regulation paper target when they were laying out the range, testing wind and real elevation. I seem to remember he did pretty good, forty-eight bulls out of fifty."

"At what range?"

"A hundred yards."

"That seems better than good to me."

"Well, yes, I guess you could say that."

"How about Rider and Calgary?"

"Both good shots. They been plinking rabbits since they were knee high."

"What's this you said about real elevation?"

"I don't know what the experts call it. That's just how it looked to me. You lay down and rest the barrel of your rifle on a mound, a little ridge, or a tripod and sight your target. Could look like it was downhill when it was really uphill or vice versa. Optical illusion. You got to calibrate the corrections."

"Well," I said, sticking out my hand to shake his hand again. "I want to thank you for your time and cooperation."

"I hope I haven't helped you put those boys deeper in the shit."

"If they stepped in it by accident, I'll be trying to get them out with their boots as clean as anybody could hope for. But if one or two of them's deliberately jumped in the pile hoping to find a gold horseshoe, well, I'll have to put that on the table too."

He nodded his head, smiled one more time, and then turned away from me as though I'd been no more than a wind passing across the land from outside the Settlement.

I left the Mesquakie Indian Settlement and drove straight down Sixty-three about a hundred and twenty-five miles. My foot ain't as heavy as some, so I reached Ottumwa in a shade under two hours, arriving at the railroad station about noon.

Kelly Primrose is the stationmaster there. He's one of those men who looks like he stepped out of an old photogravure, solemn eyes looking at you from a hundred years past, mouth pushed out like it was sucking a persimmon, thin hair combed across a round head like it was pasted there and would never stir, not even in a tornado.

"Word has it that you're out to save those Indians," he said, before we'd even said hello.

"Mostly I'm looking for the truth," I said. "Would it bother you if I got them out of the trouble they're in?"

He thought about that.

"Not so's I'd lose any sleep about it."

"But you have an interest?"

"Well, you know, my nephew was in a car wreck caused by a Mesquakie Indian driving under the influence up around Montezuma where they got that skiing. Got his leg busted in two places. Had the damndest time getting compensation. Government wards and all."

"Well, it's the government you should be mad at, not the Indians."

"You got a point there. What brings you by, Jake? Looking over the lay of the land?"

"That's right, Kelly. I wonder if I could trade you my company car for your four-wheeler for an hour or two."

"I think I can manage without it. I take my lunch at my desk."

I handed over my keys and he gave me the key to his vehicle after taking it off his key ring.

"You sure two hours'll be enough?" he asked.

"How's that?"

"Won't you be stopping by Lula Rippard's?"

"Now that you mention it, maybe I will," I said.

He grinned. It was like one of the faces on Mount

Rushmore suddenly cracking a smile. It came and went so fast you had to make an effort to remember if you'd really seen it.

"Maybe you'd do best to call first before driving on out there."

Before I could ask him what he meant by that, he left the counter and came out into the waiting room on the way to the toilets, saying, "Go ahead and use the phone on my desk if you want to," as he passed by.

I went into the office, sat down in his chair, and dialed Lula Rippard's number from memory.

"Hello, this is Lula Rippard," she said in the merry voice she had that always made me grin.

"Hello, Lula, this is Jake."

"Jake Hatch?"

"Well, how many Jakes do you know, Lula?"

"Not many, it's true, but you never know who might be calling you out of the blue, do you?"

"I guess I expected you to recognize my voice."

"Well, it's been a time, hasn't it, Jake?"

"Maybe a month, Lula. Not more than that, I don't think."

"Four weeks can be a lifetime nowadays," she said.

"I was wondering, since I took the trip down here from Marshalltown, if we could have lunch or a cup of tea together."

"My house is in an uproar."

"How about supper, then? Do you expect it'll still be in an uproar around supper time?"

"I doubt the party will last that long."

"I wouldn't mind being invited to a little party," I said.

"It's a shower. Just for ladies. I know you wouldn't mind being the only man in a bunch of women, but such gatherings are times for some serious joking and gossip and I don't think even a man with your charms would be welcome."

"One of your friends having a baby?"

"It's a wedding shower."

There was a little pause. I could hear it coming.

"My wedding, Jake."

I could hear the end of an era. I knew the sexual revolution of the sixties, seventies, and half of the eighties was over. It sounded just like a door slamming.

"Did you hear what I said, Jake?"

"I'm trying to frame a proper congratulation, Lula."

"The way it goes is congratulations to the groom and best wishes to the bride."

"The idea being that he's won a prize and she's taken on a doubtful enterprise?"

"Now, Jake, don't get quarrelsome."

"I wasn't trying to make a quarrel, Lula, I was trying to make a joke."

"Oh," she said, and laughed a short one.

"I'm going to miss you, Lula."

"I should hope so, Jake. I missed you enough."

"I'm sorry, Lula. I mean I'm happy for you getting married, if it's what you want, but I'm sorry we won't be having any good conversations over supper again."

"After my husband and I are settled in, maybe in a year or so, we could have you over some evening."

"Ah, well, Lula," I said, because I didn't have any idea how I should answer that. "Best wishes and be happy."

"You too, Jake."

I waited for her to hang up.

When Primrose came back he shot me another one of his stone-breaking grins and asked me had I contacted Lula Rippard.

"She's getting married. Did you know that?" I said.

"Well, I thought I heard something like that, but I wasn't sure," he replied, looking as innocent as a bunny rabbit.

I changed the subject by asking him to refresh my memory about the terrain where the shooting occurred.

He went over to the map on the wall and studied it for a minute. "Halfway between here and Munterville. Say eight and a half miles west of the outskirts of Ottumwa."

I thanked him and went on my way.

I drove Primrose's four-wheeler out of town and then took H Thirty-five until I was eight measured miles beyond Ottumwa's western limit, where I left the road and parked the truck in the tulles.

The pebbly, sandy dirt wasn't going to do my oxfords any good. I should've thought to bring along a pair of boots, but it was too late to worry about that.

I kicked my way over to the railroad tracks, turned around and paced off a quarter of a mile, then turned east and walked about half a mile, dragging a stick I busted off a mesquite bush behind me. Went south for another quarter of a mile, then turned west, pacing off a mile, turned north, and so forth, until I had a rectangle a mile wide and a quarter mile deep laying there scratched on the land.

I was about pooped, so I hunkered down for a little rest. After about five minutes I stood up and almost fell over with dizziness.

Your body gives you little signs like that every once in a while, telling you that you're not a youngster anymore and can't go squatting and standing up all of a sudden like that without suffering the consequences. Also the muscles in my legs were already sore right down to my thighbones.

Anyway, I started ranging that quarter of a square mile looking at the ground, bending over to knee level—with some difficulty—and running my eye along the ground every so often. I wasn't looking for a cartridge or a dent on a dune made by a rifle barrel.

I'm not that foolish. I just wanted to see if land that looked as flat as a griddle had ripples and folds in it deep enough to hide somebody laying out prone.

That's how they say the Indians used to pop up out of the ground like magic when they attacked wagon trains and columns of cavalry. Nowhere to be seen one second and swarming all over the place the next.

I was even down on my belly a dozen times. I could see how an army could be concealed on the supposedly flat land between me and the railroad tracks.

I walked back to the four-wheeler, beginning to feel the strain in my legs, thinking about the way it could've happened. How somebody could've talked the Indians into hoo-rahing the train that way while they were waiting in ambush in a fold of the land. Lying there with a marksman's rifle and heavy ammunition designed to break up and scatter. Lying there with an eye to a scope, waiting until the California Zephyr went by. Traveling west. Passengers having supper. One passenger in particular having supper at the last call, lingering over a cup of coffee.

It wasn't perfect but it was a way it could've happened.

What I had to know was:

Could you see somebody raise a glass from a quarter of a mile away?

Was Harold Chaney a man of predictable habits?

Who knew Abraham Woodman and Dan Pool so well that they could've set them up to play the beard, concealing cold-blooded murder behind what looked like drunken damn-foolishness?

What was the truth about Harold Chaney and the Whente take-over? Had he wanted it or hadn't he?

I got back to the truck, drove it to within a quarter of a mile of the tracks, parked it, stretched out in the cab, and slept.

The sun was just going down when I woke up. I sat

there getting colder until after eight when the Zephyr went through, traveling west. I could see the little squares of light in the cars. I could pick out the dining-car windows and even make out which tables had people seated at them. But there was no way I could've seen anybody raise a glass.

So how had Willy gotten that idea?

Twenty-four

I LOOKED IT UP and found out that Malcolm, Seagrave, Morrison, and Hedrick had offices in Chicago, Des Moines, Lincoln, and Denver.

A telephone call from a roadside booth to each office told me that Jack Hedrick wasn't immediately available, would I leave a name and number.

I drove back to Marshalltown wondering if Hedrick was on the job, though I doubted a partner would be doing the early donkey work, leaving things like appearances and arraignments to a junior associate.

Al Bunty looked up from his desk when I walked into the jail house and said, "Don't you keep normal hours?"

"I could ask you the same thing, Al. Looks like we're both a couple of night owls."

"There's benefits," he said.

"Maybe for you but not for me. I seem to've got my feet tangled in an after-dark investigation, like it or not."

"So, what brings you back? Want me to wake up those Indians again?"

"I don't think so. I wanted to ask you did a lawyer by the name of Jack Hedrick come talk to them?"

"There's been lawyers passing through." He opened his desk drawer and started shuffling through a mess of papers. "One of them was from the Indian Bureau." What he was looking for was floating on the top. "Then there was this one." He tossed over a calling card.

It was from Hedrick's firm but it wasn't Hedrick's card. The name on it was Philip Shanahan.

"He appear for Abe Woodman?"

"He did better than that."

"What better than that?"

"He got him released OR."

"How about Dan Pool?"

"He's been moved out of here to Des Moines."

"Rider and Calgary still in your jail?"

"Let out in custody this afternoon."

"Whose custody?"

"Jim Willows, the chief over to Mesquakie."

"I spoke to him in the morning and he didn't say anything about taking custody of those two."

"Maybe he didn't know he'd be asked."

"What were the terms of the release?"

"Just they had to stay on the reservation until the next appearance before the court."

"Where's this Shanahan now, or did he just do what he had to do and leave town?"

Bunty shrugged. "Beats me. Why don't you look in on the hotel. If he's anywhere he'll be at the bar over there."

"What makes you say that?"

"He's a man who likes his refreshment. You find him and you'll see."

He closed the desk drawer, letting me keep the card,

and got to his feet. "Doesn't happen you've got a couple more of them passes on you, does it?"

"I guess," I said, and wrote him out another pair.

I walked over to the hotel. The woman in the summer dress showing off her legs was still there. So was the fella who ran the hardware store and the other who looked like an undertaker. He waved to me like he was an old friend and I waved back. The bartender started over as I looked around. I spotted Beecher sitting in the same booth in which we sat the night before. There was somebody sitting with him.

"Send a rye and branch over to that table, will you?" I said. "And bring Mr. Beecher one of his ginger ales and the other fella whatever he's been having."

"Double whiskeys with a beer back."

"If that's what he wants," I said, and walked on over.

Beecher was facing me and saw me coming. He smiled and raised a hand.

"Hello, Jake. I didn't expect to see you so soon again," Beecher said.

"I ordered you another ginger ale, is that okay?" I said.

"Sure. Sit down and shake hands with Phil Shanahan." He slid over in the booth to make room for me.

"Phil Shanahan, Jake Hatch," Beecher said.

We shook hands all around.

I could see right away what Bunty meant about Shanahan being a drinker. He was a big man with a puffy face and hands, which could've been the result of alcoholic edema. Sitting there, he looked like he'd just finished running a footrace, his complexion so red it threatened to bleed out of his pores. The blood vessels in his nose had given up and busted by the hundreds. His red hair was going pink.

I decided not to play pussyfoot. "Which office of

Malcolm, Seagrave, Morrison, and Hedrick do you work out of?"

His eyebrows popped up two inches and he grinned as though I'd just asked him if he still beat his wife.

"That's a pretty big firm," I said. "Are you a partner?"

The eyebrows crawled up another inch but he still didn't say anything.

"I hope you don't mind," I said. "I bought you a drink."

The bartender arrived with them just then. Shanahan grabbed hold of the fresh double shot as though he feared somebody'd snatch it away from him.

He could be had cheap. He was already willing to answer simple questions for the price of a double boilermaker.

"Just a senior associate," he said, in a plummy English accent, which was a little ragged around the edges. "I was a solicitor, not a barrister, in England. It's taken me a little time to pass the bar and settle in, so I'm a late starter with expectations, shall we say."

"You did a good job, I hear," I said.

"Good job about what?"

"About getting Abraham Woodman out of jail. How come nobody could do the same for Dan Pool?"

"Well, a case like this gets to be a jurisdictional mess. Two juveniles have to be tried separately. Two reservation Indians have to be treated with special care."

"Woodman and Dan Pool claim to be reservation Indians out of the Santee."

"Get my point? That's in Nebraska. Not even another county, but another state."

"They're not Santee Sioux. They're Cheyenne. Probably from the Carolinas," Beecher said.

"Oh, for bloody Christ's sake," Shanahan said, like

he was disgusted with the whole thing, and batted back the double in one toss.

"No matter what they are, no matter how they fool around with jurisdictions and agencies," I said, "somebody's got to be tried for the killing, accidental or otherwise"—Shanahan reacted to that—"and what I'm wondering is, who's scattering these people all over the landscape and confusing the issue and how come the state's attorney isn't making it tougher on you defense lawyers?"

"Well, I don't know," Shanahan said. "What do you think?"

"You ever watch a cowboy cut a steer out of the herd or a shepherd send out his dog to isolate a sheep for slaughter?"

"Is that what you think's going on?" Beecher asked.

"It's a thought."

"Which sheep do you think they're isolating?"

"I wish I knew."

"Let me stand you a drink," Shanahan said, sticking up his arm to get the bartender's attention.

"I'm still good," I said.

"Three's my limit," Beecher said, smiling.

"Well, I'd better have another," Shanahan said. "I don't like to see friends of mine drinking alone."

"Did you know Harold Chaney?" I asked.

"Naturally," Shanahan said, brightening up somewhat because I'd given him the chance to show he was given chances to serve important clients and might not be such an insignificant employee of Malcolm, Seagrave, Morrison, and Hedrick after all.

"What kind of a man would you say he was?"

"You can't get more general than that, can you?" he said, chiding me.

"Well, maybe I can't get any more particular than that. The only time I ever saw the man, he was dead."

"Chaney was like practically every other man who

makes his pile on his own. Well, maybe not on his own, but by seeing the opportunity inherent in somebody else's idea and riding it to the top."

"You mean Lewis Warden's discoveries about alloys?"

"Yes, that."

"Chaney'd made a pile before that."

"Small change compared to what he was able to acquire after he teamed up with Warden."

"I get the feeling Warden got the short end of the deal."

"That's the way it might seem. The financial side of companies are always more important than the production side. Raising expansion money, administrating sales, that's where American industry has placed the emphasis."

"That's why it's in such trouble," Beecher said.

Shanahan nodded. "Go tell it to the stock market. That's where the real fortunes are made. Selling paper."

I didn't really want to get into a discussion of real industrial values and castles made of stock certificates.

"So Chaney was ruthless?" I said.

"There's a word. Most people call somebody ruthless just because they saw an opportunity and were willing to do what was needed to exploit it. Just because somebody grabs the bull by the horns and drops it on its back."

"And shortchanges other people?"

"People who would not have known how to make the thing profitable themselves? Why not?"

Shanahan was trying to give us the impression that he could be such a man except for having a soft heart and a basic lack of interest.

If you pay attention, you'll see how often people will talk to you or answer a question in an awkward way because they're trying to weave something self-serving into the talk or answer. It throws what they have to say slightly lopsided, like a fence leaning in the wind.

"So, he wasn't a very likable man?" I asked, just to keep the motor turning over.

"Likable, unlikable. It doesn't signify. Chaney did everything full out. Closing a deal, settling a dispute, arranging a hundred-million-dollar loan, giving time to his club, busting clay pigeons, looking for a wife or a little something on the side—"

He stopped like he'd swallowed his tongue. He was being unprofessionally indiscreet about a client, dead or otherwise, and he knew it. He was full of rage and envy and disappointment and self-disgust and whiskey. Right there, in front of strangers, his face collapsed for a second—I thought he was going to bust out crying—and I knew he didn't give a damn what confidences he gave up. He had a personal reason for disliking Chaney. I knew he wouldn't tell me what it was. I also knew I'd find out on my own, sooner or later.

"For Christ's sake, who the hell are you?" Shanahan said.

"I'm a detective working for the Burlington Northern," I said.

"Worried about a lawsuit being brought against your railroad?" he said, trying to make it an insult, but the sneer wouldn't stay put on his mouth.

"Wondering what the hell's going on."

"Me too," he said. "Getting the venue changed, the charges tailored, and the trials separated went off without a hitch. Practically no objection from the state prosecutor's office."

He made it sound as though it was a surprise to him too, but he was clumsy about it, and I'd bet he wasn't surprised at all.

"How do the charges against Dan Pool and Abe Woodman read now?"

"Simple manslaughter."

"Somebody peddling influence?"

"Now, just how the hell would I know that, Detective?"

Twenty-five

I DROVE TO OSCEOLA and dropped the company car off at the station. Even though it was the wee hours of the morning and even though I could've called one lady friend or another and begged a mug of hot chocolate and a pillow—on the couch if not in bed—and even though I was so tired I was about to put toothpicks under my eyelids to prop them open, I hitched a ride on a freight that was just leaving the yards for Denver.

"You red-balling it?" I asked the brakeman, Aldus Gifford.

"No stops till Denver," he said, and invited me into his caboose.

It was a perfect little home, complete with two built-in bunks, a rocking chair, a desk with a reading and writing lamp, and a potbellied stove on the top of which a pot of beans and bacon and a pot of coffee were keeping hot.

"Bread in the box," Gifford said. "Make yourself a bean sandwich while I walk the wheels if you want."

"I'll just sit down here on the bunk and take my shoes off. You've got the life here, you know that, Aldus?"

"Tell me about it when I get back," he said, and went off to do his service for the train.

By the time he got back, by the time the engines started pulling the train out of the yards, I guess I'd fallen asleep, because the next thing I knew, it was coming up dawn and I was lying flat on the bunk under three blankets, my head on a pillow which smelled of cinders and tobacco smoke.

Gifford was in the rocking chair reading a book by the light of the lamp, which he'd swiveled on its neck so it brightened the page without getting into my eyes.

I cleared my throat and he looked at me over the top of his spectacles, a character right out of a Norman Rockwell painting. All of a sudden I wanted to cry for my lost youth and innocence.

"Awake, are you?" he said.

"Sorry about that. I wasn't much company last night."

"You were tuckered."

I sat up and slid my legs out from under the covers and put my feet on the floor. He'd taken my shoes off.

"You need a pair of fresh socks?" he asked. "I always carry a couple pair extra." He pointed to a little cabinet at the foot of the bed.

"Thank you kindly, Aldus," I said, leaning over to look inside the cabinet and get a pair of sweat socks.

He ducked his head as though getting thanked embarrassed him.

"You married, Aldus? Funny I never asked."

"I was married. Thirty years."

"She pass away?"

"No, she left me. Well, I mean to say, she asked me to use the door."

"After thirty years?" I said, in some dismay.

He smiled softly, as though remembering good times and small pleasures. "She was a good wife to me while it lasted."

I stripped off my soiled socks and got my toes into Gifford's nice fresh ones. "Well, how come she cut you off that way? She catch you sampling along the right-of-way?"

"Oh no, nothing like that."

"You didn't take to the bottle?"

"Not that, either."

"Then she just got tired of spending so many nights alone while you were on the job."

"Other way around."

"How's that?"

"I hurt my hip jumping off a moving freight. Laid up for a month and walking around with a cane for two more. It was the longest I'd ever been home every day at one stretch."

"That upset her?"

"She said she never realized how much she enjoyed her peace and quiet."

"You're not a talker, Aldus."

"Well, it seems I snore. She could stand it a couple of nights at a time but week after week was getting too much for her."

"You could've slept with a tennis ball sewed to the back of your pajamas."

"I mentioned that. She said it might help the snoring, but her eyes had been opened to the fact that when I retired, which ain't too far down the road, she'd have to face living with me day in and day out for the rest of our lives. Just didn't see how she could stand that. Thought it best to make the break sooner instead of later."

"It upset you much?"

Gifford thought about that for a minute.

"I'll tell you, Jake, I'm one of those people sort of takes things as they come. I don't often make a fuss."

"But did you like it better being married, or do you like it better the way you are now?"

He thought about that too.

"They're different."

"I know that."

"Well, that's all I can say. How about I open the back door and you can watch the sun come up and chase us?"

So I got myself a dish of beans and bacon, and poured myself a cup of coffee, and sat there facing east in the caboose traveling west, while Gifford read his book and smoked his pipe and the dawn broke over Nebraska, thinking as how traveling by caboose was the only way to go by train nowadays.

When we pulled into Denver, Gifford put aside his book, shook my hand, thanked me for the company, and hopped off as the train slowed down almost to a stop.

I sat there for a couple of minutes thinking that Gifford had been married all those years but when the time came to be on his own it looked like he'd taken to it like a duck to water. I'd been more or less alone all my adult life, but I wondered if I couldn't take to marriage just as easy.

Twenty-six

"YOU MARRIED?" HARRIET LAWRY said. "It'd be like trying to teach a pig to swim."

The last time I'd walked in on Harriet unexpectedly, she'd been standing in the middle of her studio naked, rosy-gold in the light coming through the skylight, painting a nude of herself and surrounded by a lot of little nude sculptures.

Now she was sitting on the floor on the mattress she used for a couch and a bed, wearing a caftan which covered her like a tent, me not knowing what she was wearing underneath.

"So, you think it's something you've got to learn?"

"I think it's something you've got to have a talent for. And I don't think you've got a talent for it any more than I do."

"Maybe we just never've had a reason powerful enough."

"You mean like falling in love?"

"I'm not sure I've ever been able to work out a definition of love that satisfies me."

"Me neither. Whatever it is, I'm not sure it's best served by monogamy, or even fidelity."

"We're faced with other considerations."

"The plague."

"You mean AIDS?"

"I mean the plague. It may be worse than most human beings have suffered through the ages, but it's still a plague like bubonic or syphilis or smallpox. You know how native populations were decimated, how they died by the thousands, when the Europeans spread things like German measles, or whooping cough, or the common cold among the Eskimos?"

"Here's a plague, though, that a person can avoid just by taking a healthy mate and not roaming around anymore."

"Some of those other plagues could be avoided by jumping down into a hole. We are what we are, Jake, and I'm not going to turn my head backwards on my neck just to have a safe partner waiting at the ready. How long do you think that'd last? Reasonable precautions, Jake. Reasonable precautions."

She reached over to the little table next to the bed, opened the drawer, dipped her hand in, and came out with five or six packets of condoms.

"What we've got here is the next best thing to fidelity or abstinence."

"I haven't used one of them things since I was a boy carrying one around so long it made a permanent dent in my wallet."

"And probably weakened and broke the first time you used it. These are fresh from the drugstore." She held them out flat on her palm. "Well, go ahead, take your pick."

"It's getting a little cold-blooded, don't you think?"

"Go on, take one, and I'll show you how to put it on, and when you're ready I'll act like you surprised me."

Twenty-seven

IT MUST LOOK LIKE I was taking my sweet old time looking for the killer of Harold Chaney. Well, I've got to point out again, that nobody but me thought very strongly that it was deliberate murder. Karen Olliphant maybe hoped it was because it'd make a better story for her six o'clock report or maybe even a special, but she didn't really believe it was murder yet.

She was ready to give me a little help. I'd asked her at the funeral home, after Jessica had reacted the way she had to the woman walking past the doorway, if she'd use her sources to find out when and where Marla Kassabian had worked for Harold Chaney and where she was working and living now. But that's all I asked her to do, since I still had nothing but a wild suspicion.

The case against the Indians was getting busted up into little pieces.

The whole matter wasn't really of any serious concern to the railroad unless somebody decided to bring a civil suit for damages against them. Which, since nobody had done anything of the kind, in this most litigious of times, in this most litigious of nations, gave them no reason to be concerned but gave me one of the strongest reasons to keep on thinking that Chaney had, indeed, been shot on purpose.

I called Karen from Harriet's studio and she told me Marla Kassabian had worked for Harold Chaney as his personal secretary ten years ago, just about the time when Chaney Enterprises took off, the first Mrs. Chaney died, and he took Florence as his second wife.

Karen had an address on Marla in a quiet residential part of Denver, mostly old apartment houses that had been going condo for the last five or six years.

She wasn't working at the present time as far as Karen could find out.

I sat there on Harriet's couch, staring at one of her paintings, thinking should I call first, should I not call first before going over to Marla Kassabian's, when Harriet said, "You know, you got me thinking last night, Jake."

"About what?"

"About you and marriage."

I didn't ask her what about it.

"About me and marriage," she went on.

I got up and started putting my small belongings into the pockets of my pants and jacket, acting busy all of a sudden like I had places to go and things to do that couldn't wait.

"We're neither of us getting any younger, Jake, the plague aside."

"We'll have to save this conversation for later, Harriet. I'm off to look into this business which could be murder."

"If you have to stay on in Omaha, I don't think I'd much mind living there for a few years. As long as I could keep this place here in Denver, that is."

I suppose that all the time I was on the phone to Karen, Harriet had been standing in front of her easel with a bunch of brushes in her hand, thinking about us getting married.

I went over and kissed her on the cheek. "I'll take you out for lunch if I get through in time."

I was at the door before she called me.

"Jake," she said, "are you afraid of marriage?"

One thing I can't understand about women. Why is it they always accuse a man of being afraid of getting married instead of asking him if he'd just prefer not to? It's like they're trying to challenge his courage, which I think is very underhanded, even sly.

"You can decide the place," I said, as though I was too preoccupied to even hear what she'd said.

Marla Kassabian's condominium was in a nice old brick four-story building. The vestibule had the original marble floors, which had been kept up very well, and the bank of brass mailboxes were original. Each one had a mouthpiece so visitors could tell the people they were visiting who they were. The door was on a buzzer.

I thought about waiting around until somebody came out and I could slip through and I thought about wandering around back to see if there was a way in through the basement or the laundry room but finally I decided to play it very straight and not try to frighten or fool the woman.

I pressed the bell and a minute later a woman's voice asked who was there.

"My name's Jake Hatch. I wanted to talk to you at Harold Chaney's funeral but I didn't get the chance."

"I didn't attend Mr. Chaney's funeral," she said.

I didn't dispute it. If she wanted to deny it, that was okay with me.

"I still have a few questions. I'm a detective for the

railroad. I can show you my badge and credentials at the door so you'll know you've got nothing to be afraid of."

"All right, come up," she said. "I'm buzzing now."

She lived on the top floor. The elevator was old and bumped a little but it didn't take forever to get there.

There were four apartments on each floor. She was standing in the open door of one of them, standing back in the shadows. I couldn't be sure she was the woman I'd seen at the funeral home. Women can change their appearance in a dozen easy ways. She shifted. Light from a skylight above her head struck her hair and it blazed like a smoldering fire.

I couldn't see her right arm but I could tell her hand was raised and resting on something inside.

"Ms. Kassabian?"

"Mrs.," she said. "I've got nothing against Mrs."

I took out my badge case and flipped it open.

She didn't even glance at it, she just kept on looking at my face, making up her mind. Then she stepped back and opened the door all the way. "Come in, Mr. Hatch."

There was an antique wardrobe against the wall on the right-hand side of the door. I glanced at it as I stepped inside and she closed the door. I had a feeling there was a handgun on top of the piece of furniture, behind the cornice.

She walked in front of me, looking back over her shoulder at me and then at the cornice. She smiled like she'd read my mind. She was wearing a green dress that set off the color of her hair. It fit her very affectionately around hips that were just going to plump.

The living room was one of the nicest rooms I'd ever seen in a city apartment. Fruitwood furniture and overstuffed chairs upholstered in sprays of green leaves, a rug on the floor the color of grass with wild flowers in it. The English china lamps had pale green watered-silk shades. There were porcelain figurines on the side tables that looked like they were almost alive. It was like a stage setting designed for her hair.

"Please sit down," she said, and sat down herself, crossing her legs at the ankles and catching her skirt underneath her thighs. She was ripe in the way that some women get in those last couple of years before middle age or old age or whatever you want to call it starts taking some of the juice out of them. It's like a fruit tree flowering with a vengeance one last time.

"What makes you think I was at the funeral, Mr. Hatch?"

"Jessica Chaney thought that a red-haired woman, wearing a mink coat, was you. Then she decided it wasn't."

"But you thought she was lying?"

"I thought there was a chance she was right the first time."

"I don't own a mink coat, Mr. Hatch."

"You worked for Mr. Chaney for quite a while?"

"I was his confidential secretary for more than eight years."

"With him from the beginning?"

"As near the beginning, when he found he had need of one, as doesn't matter."

"Why did you leave his employ?"

"His second wife, Florence, disapproved of me. She made his life difficult."

"Why did she disapprove of you?"

"She suspected that our relationship was not entirely professional."

"Was she right?"

"We'd become lovers some months after his first wife became ill."

I guess I must've frowned a little.

"Can't hardly get secretaries that conscientious

nowadays, can you?" she said, making a rowdy joke out of it, laughing at me without cracking a smile. "I think it started because I had red hair and his wife had red hair. Not the same color, but a shade of red. Harold had a thing about redheads."

"The present Mrs. Chaney has brown hair."

She smiled.

"The first Mrs. Chaney didn't object to the arrangement?"

"She encouraged it. She couldn't accommodate Harold. He was a vigorous man."

I had pictures of Harold Chaney and Marla Kassabian going at it on the desk in his office or scrambling around, skirt up and trousers down, on the rug.

She laughed briefly and artificially, reading my mind again.

"Would you like something to drink? A glass of sherry?"

"I'm fine, thank you. When his wife died, was your relationship outside the office still going on?"

"Oh yes."

"Then why . . ."

"Why didn't Harold marry me?"

I nodded.

She got up from her chair and walked over to the window, pushing the sheer curtains aside and gazing down at the crown of a linden tree.

"I had no money."

"Beg pardon."

She turned around and I could see old anger and hurt in her eyes.

"I had no money. Florence had plenty. And brown hair." She smiled again. "Harold needed it for the big expansion he had planned. The giant step. 'The one chance only,' he called it. It wasn't the only chance. He could have found the money elsewhere when the business had grown, but Harold didn't want to wait.

He was an impatient man. God, he was an impatient man."

It was like the punch line to an old burlesque joke, and she got it the same time I got it. Her face did funny things trying to work it off, struggling with remorse, grief, pain, dignity, and bawdy laughter. The bawdy laughter won.

We sat there laughing like a couple of Laurel and Hardy fans.

Sharing knock-down, flat-out, nothing-held-back belly laughs with another person makes them an instant friend. Maybe it's because when you're rolling around and slapping your knees, you're pretty helpless, and somehow the primitive brain inside your civilized mind knows that you could've been killed while you were laughing and the other person didn't kill you so you can trust them forever after that. I don't know, but that's the way it could work.

When we got our breath back and wiped away our tears, me with the heel of my hand and she with her little handkerchief, we looked at each other and smiled.

"Thank God for laughter," she said.

"It keeps us from going crazy," I said.

"So, all right, I wasn't quite the woman spurned. Harry was all very straightforward about what he wanted and intended. He said he didn't expect to get certain things from Florence and, letting me know he was happy in our relationship and wanted it to continue, he offered an arrangement."

"A contract for services?"

"Harold was a precise man. He was in love with time lines and schedules. He liked doing the same things in the same way, at the same time, day after day and year after year. He liked to put things in pigeon-holes and keep them there. I suppose being so predictable in small things freed him to be unpredictable in big things."

"You accepted the arrangement?"

She gestured at the room filled with expensive furniture and collectibles. "If I was going to be a kept woman, I intended to do it right. Very European. Very French. Nothing careless or casual about it. A commitment in its own way just as powerful, just as sacred, just as demanding as marriage vows."

She got up and went over to a black lacquered cabinet that opened up into a bar at the touch of her finger. "We should have a little something," she said. "Rye whiskey good for you?"

"Just a tad."

"Three-finger tad?"

"Two'll do."

"Straight up, on the rocks, or over the stones?"

"Straight up."

She talked as she made the drinks, pouring her whiskey into a glass of ice to chill it and then decanting it into another glass so sitting in cubes wouldn't water it down.

"If Harry wasn't ready to offer me the ultimate security of marriage—since I wouldn't have the protection of the law—I laid down my terms. The lease on this apartment, a new car every third year, a salary as a consultant though I never consulted—not exactly —shares in Chaney Enterprises, and more shares each year our relationship continued. Other considerations."

"So you left his employment?"

"I said I did. Six months after he married Florence."

"Did she know about your new contract? Did she know that Chaney had moved you out of the office into . . ."

"A love nest?" She filled in for me when I hesitated a second. "I like that. It sounds like something out of a Restoration comedy."

She came back and handed me my drink, then set hers on the end table next to her chair and sat down again. "Rye and a bone."

"Where'd you learn the lingo?"

"I was never a barmaid but I've perched on a stool in many a bar on many an afternoon." She tilted her head and added, "I'm not a lush, Jake."

"Was Harold Chaney unfaithful to you?"

"You mean besides being unfaithful to his wife was he unfaithful to me?" She didn't expect an answer. "You know about the study on the ram and the ewes?"

"Ma'am?" I said, wondering how sheep got into the conversation.

"Don't do that," she said, very sharp and quick. "Calling me ma'am makes me sound old. Or it makes me think you're trying to sound old-fashioned and homey and there's no reason for either of us to turn into horse traders here. I'll tell you what I want to tell you, which will probably be as much as you want to know."

"Sorry."

"Don't mind me. I'm on a hair trigger. Losing a lover through death makes you think about yourself and the years going by. It makes you nervous and hungry for . . ."

She stopped as though she'd just that second realized she wasn't talking to herself but to a man sitting two arm-lengths away from her. I knew what she meant. The sexual appetite gets very instant in some people after they've been around death. Widows have been known to make love to the undertaker in sight of the coffin and widowers have been known to proposition the nurses who just came into the living room to declare the wife dead.

"About the ram and the ewes?" I said.

"They discovered in this one study I read about that if you put a ram to the same ewe in consecutive couplings, he loses interest and won't perform the fourth and sometimes even the third time. Put the same ram to a succession of ewes and he'll keep performing until he drops from exhaustion. So the trick in keeping some men is letting them have plenty of slack, plenty of opportunity for playtime with new playmates."

"Did he have a new playmate?"

"Several, I'd imagine."

"One in particular?"

"I wouldn't know about that."

"One he called Pip?"

Her eyes got narrow the way a cat's do when it's disturbed or angry. Her jaw clenched like she was biting down on something sour. And her throat and cheeks colored up. It only lasted a few seconds and was almost all gone when she turned her head away and set down her glass.

"The only Pip I know about is the one in Dickens' *Great Expectations.*"

"That was a boy."

"I know."

"I was told he used to call his wife, Elizabeth, Pip," I said.

"I'd forgotten about that," she said softly.

"One more thing, Mrs. Kassabian."

"Yes?"

"Do you know how to fire a rifle as well as a handgun?"

"I'm a better than average shot with any kind of firearm," she said, looking at me without a flicker of an eyelash.

I finished my drink and stood up.

"Want another?" she asked.

I had a feeling that another could lead to another could lead to the bedroom, but either all the talk of plague or a natural reluctance about taking advantage of somebody so vulnerable or the thought that, having lost one provider, she might be looking for another, decided me to be on my way.

"I've got a lot of things to do today. Maybe some other time."

She stood up and walked with me to the door where she paused with her hand on the latch long enough to tell me, "There won't be another time, Jake. A man like yourself should know that a woman opens a window of opportunity and if a man doesn't do something about it she probably won't open it again."

Twenty-eight

EVERY TIME I TALKED to somebody new, instead of narrowing down the field of suspects, it seemed like I kept adding to them.

I called George McGilvray in Akron and asked him if he had any time to talk it out with me. I could drive the hundred and twelve miles from Denver and after our conference I could drive the thirty-four miles back to Fort Morgan and catch the 10:25 P.M. to Chicago. George said he'd do me one better and meet me in Fort Morgan so I didn't have to go driving back and forth. I said I'd buy him dinner, and Bess, too, if she cared to come along. We arranged to meet at a steak house I favored where you got your choice of three cuts of steak, a ground beef dinner, or chicken.

The reason I wanted to talk to George was because he was the best law enforcement officer I know. He might not ever have been the detective that Silas Spinks once was, but Silas was my boss and if I started talking the situation over with him, he'd tell me it was getting too complicated to be worth the trouble and order me to step out of it.

When I got to the restaurant in Fort Morgan, George and Bess were already waiting for me. They were sitting at the table nearest the window. He was staring at the foam in the glass of beer in front of him and she was fiddling with the pencil they give you to mark off your order on preprinted checks.

Almost before I had a chance to sit down, he looked up at me and said, "How come you're bothering with this one, Jake? You're logging a lot of miles and a lot of hours."

"The only thing I can say," I replied, kissing Bess on the cheek, catching the waiter's eye, and pointing to George's glass of beer, meaning I'd have the same, "is that the people in this killing are spread all over the map from Denver to Chicago, from Ottumwa up to the Santee Reservation on the Nebraska–Dakota border. Somebody could get away with murder just because there's so damn many agencies and jurisdictions involved in this.

"The homicide occurred outside Ottumwa but they detached the car from the train further west at Osceola, so it's the Osceola police who secure the crime scene and the Clarke County sheriffs who come to take jurisdiction. They send a medical examiner down from Des Moines, but that's all right, local facilities couldn't handle it very well."

George just nodded, having heard most or all of this before, as the waiter came over and set down two beers. He waited to see if George was going to drink off what was left in his first but George waved him away.

"Have you changed your mind, ma'am?" the waiter asked.

"Perhaps I'll have a Dubonnet and soda," Bess said.

"Would you like to order now?" the waiter asked.

"We'll send up a rocket," George said.

After the waiter walked away I said, "Local police and county sheriffs looked for the bullet or what was left of it."

"Did they ever find anything?" George asked.

"See what I mean? I've been running around so much I never even checked on that."

"Well, if they had, they would've told you."

"The men they arrest turn out to be Indians, which means the Bureau gets into it one way or another."

"About the Indians?" Bess said.

"Information I get one place turns out not to be true somewhere else down the line."

"Like what?"

"Like Atterbury, the sheriff over to Clarke County, told me none of the Indians came from Mesquakie but were only visiting, but it turns out two of them do and two of them who claim to be Santee Reservation Sioux work at Mesquakie but live off the reservation. But that's not the worst. The biggest bother is they keep splitting those Indians up and moving them around."

"You getting hungry?" George asked. "I'm getting hungry."

"Okay, send up the rocket."

I marked off a sirloin rare, baked potato, and apple pie. Everything else came with it.

"Same way they do it on the trains," I said. "Marking it off. I suppose it's easier, but it lacks something."

"It's the plastic they serve on in the dining cars that makes me want to cry," Bess said.

We sat there staring at each other for a minute, thinking about all the things you lose with progress, while the waiter collected the orders.

"The Indians?" Bess said again.

"First all six of them were jailed at Indianola. Then

I'm told they'd been moved up to Marshalltown. When I go to see them there, the two youngest have been moved over to Grand Rapids. After a lawyer named Phil Shanahan—from a big law firm representing Abraham Woodman, one of the Indians—gets into it, the Indians from Mesquakie get set loose in their chief's custody, Woodman gets out on his own recognizance, and this other one, Dan Pool, gets sent to Des Moines."

"Maybe they're moving them around because ugly rumors are starting to fly," George said.

"You mean ugly rumors of lynching mobs and things like that? Well, there aren't any such ugly rumors. Nobody seems to give much of a damn. The papers and the television aren't playing it up. It looks like the story's just fallen between the cracks."

"So, they're moving the one most likely up to Des Moines because it's the capital and the state attorney is taking the case."

"I'm wondering could it be he's being moved into bigger and tougher facilities which end up being run as much by the prisoners as the guards. Where a man can get killed in a quarrel over nothing."

"My God, you've got an imagination, Jake. You start off with an accidental shooting and now it's a major conspiracy to commit murder, not once but twice, and you've got somebody with enough clout to move these Indians around like they were checkers on a board."

"You yourself said it would take more gun than those Indians had to fire the shot that killed Chaney."

"I said *probably*. Get it straight."

"Nothing's straight in this damn business."

The waiter brought our dinners. We were quiet while we ate for a little.

"Then there's the emerald ring," I said.

"Emerald ring?"

"The five-carat whopper Chaney had on him when he was killed."

"Present for his wife?"

"Not her birthday anytime soon and no holidays coming up. Not for his mother. She doesn't like emeralds. Not for his daughter. Not the type for a flashy piece like that, too young to carry it off. Doesn't look like she wears rings anyhow. Besides, he had it in his pocket going west and it was inscribed inside with a name none of the Chaney women is called but which Chaney once called his first wife."

"What name?" George asked.

"Pip."

"That leaves the mistress," Bess said.

"I didn't tell you about any mistress."

"A five-carat emerald? There's a mistress."

"I thought that was the case at first. She's got this red hair and wears green dresses and decorates her apartment in green because it sets her hair off so fine."

Bess nodded. "That's the color I'd favor if I were a redhead."

"How'd you get Pip out of her given name, Marla Kassabian?" I wondered.

"I called George Pooh Bear the first two years we were married. How would you get that out of George McGilvray?"

"You ask her about this name Pip?" George asked.

"I did."

"How did she react?"

"With anger."

"How's that?"

"I asked her if Harold Chaney called her by a pet name and she said no. I asked her did he ever call her Pip and her eyes got narrow, her jaw clenched, and her neck and cheeks colored up."

"Oh-oh," Bess said.

I knew right then what she was going to say next.

"It looks to me that there was a mistress all right," Bess said. "In fact, there are probably two. An old one and a new one."

"So, if we forget about it being a business rival or someone who might be hurt if Chaney Enterprises were sold off or not sold off, as the case may be, it could be one of three women. The wife, the long-time mistress, or a new one we suspect might be standing in the wings."

"Or might not even exist," George said, as though trying to be the voice of reason.

"One of them shot Harold Chaney or arranged to have him shot by a hired hand."

"I vote for one of the ladies," Bess said, almost cheerfully. Then she added, with one of her quirky smiles, "Should be a lesson in there for you, Jake. One woman at a time is the surest way to live a long and healthy life."

Twenty-nine

I SLEPT IN THE dormitory car all the way to Mount Pleasant, Iowa, where I had to rent a car, since no company cars were available, and drove the hundred and fifteen miles to Cedar Rapids where they were keeping Willy and Charlie in the juvenile facility there.

I had a little trouble convincing the head honcho that my business with the youngsters was not only legitimate but could well clear up what I believed to be the murder of Harold Chaney. I had to remind her of who Harold Chaney was. How many manufacturers or industrialists do any of us remember? Even ones that get shot in the head while dining on a train.

We get the idea in our heads that whatever we're interested in at the moment is something everybody else is interested in too. We forget how quickly today's news becomes tomorrow's garbage can liner.

So I had some talking to do, but finally she said

okay, I could have a talk with the boys. Did I want to see them one at a time or both at once?

I said one at a time and I went to wait in a room with grates on the windows and an automatic lock on the door until the first one was delivered to me.

There was a plain wooden table and four straight-backed wooden chairs in the room. Nothing else.

The guard opened the door and Charlie came shuffling in. He was a skinny, chicken-breasted kid, with a cocked eye and no chin, the product of careless prenatal care—if any—and bad nutrition when he was a baby.

I could tell he felt lost and vulnerable without his friend Willy and without the company of the older men.

"You remember me, Charlie?" I asked.

"I know who you are."

"So, sit down and let's have a little chat."

"I don't know what we got to chat about," he said, but he sat down across from me anyway.

"I wonder why they split you men up," I said.

"Willy and me ain't eighteen yet."

"That's true. But . . ."

"But what?" he asked, when I hesitated.

"I was just thinking. In cases of capital crimes juveniles can be tried as adults."

"Capital crimes?"

"Murder, for one."

His eyes got big for a second and he made a sound in his throat as though he was going to be sick. "Jesus Christ," he whispered.

"You don't act surprised," I said.

"What do you mean, I don't act surprised."

"Well, I mention the fact that we could be looking at murder here and that you could maybe be charged with it—"

"What the hell you talking about?" he said, his

voice getting high and thin. "Why would anybody charge me with killing that man?"

"You and Willy both."

He turned his head aside, the way an animal under attack will sometimes do, trying to see if a step out of danger will invite a blow. But there was no place to run and he knew it. His eyes turned sly. I could see him working it out.

"Willy maybe knows something I don't know about what happened, but I swear to God I didn't have no idea what was going on."

"So, something was going on?"

"I just said I didn't know anything when we went out and drove alongside the train. Hell, I wasn't the first one to take a shot at it. I wouldn't have shot at it at all, except everybody else was shooting at it."

"Let's keep our eye on the mark, will we, Charlie? You said you had no idea what was going on?"

"That's right."

"So, what makes you think, now, there was something going on?"

"Well, after we shot at the train for a couple of miles, we stopped."

"What do you mean, you stopped?"

"We just stopped. Whoever was driving the trucks . . ."

"Woodman and Rider."

"Yeah, Woodman and Rider just turned away and drove up onto the highway and started back to Tama."

"Who broke it off first?"

"What?"

"Who drove up out of the tulles toward the highway first, Rider or Woodman?"

"Abe did. He was in the first truck."

"Refresh my memory. Abe Woodman was driving Willy's truck, Willy was sitting next to him, and Calgary was in the back."

Charlie was a slow thinker but he left the impression that what he finally decided to tell you was the truth as best he knew it. "No, no. I don't think so. I think Dan Pool was riding in the back of Willy's truck. I'm positive Calgary was riding in the back of my truck."

"How come you didn't go back to Wahoo?"

"What?"

I repeated the question. I knew I was going to get a "What?" for every question I asked that wasn't in a straight line from the question before. It gave him a little extra time to think.

"Why would we go back to Wahoo?"

"Well, to celebrate the good time you'd just had. To go back to the rib joint."

"Nobody was hungry anymore," he said, innocently. "We just wanted to go home."

"Is that what you all did?"

"We went back to the Silver Saddle Saloon in Tama first to sort out who needed a ride where."

"And something happened there that made you think all that hootin' and hollerin' wasn't something that didn't just happen because of too much beer and the natural exuberance of young men?"

"There was somebody waiting for us in the parking lot at the Silver Saddle."

"How do you know it was somebody waiting for you?"

"I don't mean for me in particular. I mean for some of us in the crowd."

"Some of you?"

"Well, a couple. Jesus Christ, I don't know how many she was waiting for. I thought it was maybe a girlfriend of Dan Pool's or maybe Abe's."

"A woman?"

"That's right. A woman in a nineteen-eighty-four Cadillac Seville. Dark green with red pinstriping."

"How'd you know it was a woman?"

"I heard her call when we got out of the trucks. We were going in for one last beer and then we were going to see—"

"Who needed a ride home."

"That's right."

"Did you see her face?"

"No, she didn't get out of the car. Dan Pool and Abe Woodman walked over to her car."

"Then what?"

"She handed Dan Pool something. Abe tried to pull him away but Dan Pool told him to get away. Then he saw the rest of us watching and told us to get the hell inside the saloon, it was none of our business."

"So you all did what he said?"

"Dan Pool can be very mean when he wants to be. It's best not to cross him. It was none of my business, so I did what he said."

"The rest go in with you?"

"Sure. Except Willy took his good old time about it. He don't like to be told what to do."

"Did Dan Pool and Woodman come in after a while?"

"Abe did. I didn't ask but I figured Dan Pool had gone off with his lady friend."

"Okay, Charlie, I guess that's all I've got to ask you now."

"You think I'm going to be charged with murder?" Charlie asked.

I couldn't put his mind to rest because I still had Willy to talk to and I didn't want Charlie telling him I was running a bluff, so I just shrugged and said, "We'll just have to see."

"It'd be bad, you know," he said. "People don't like Indians around here."

Thirty

WILLY LOOKED LIKE HE'D be a much tougher nut to crack, but Willy was a young boy trying to act like a man. He had a four-wheel truck, rifles in an overhead rack, and older men let him buddy around and even drink with them. He was as tangle-footed and eager as a puppy. Loyal to a fault.

"Your pa know about the trouble you're in?" I asked.

"My pa's a drunk. He don't know where I am and he wouldn't give a damn if he did," he said defiantly. But underneath the show was a bid for sympathy.

"Maybe he figures you're a man and responsible for what you do."

"Okay, let's say that."

"How about your mother?"

"Dead."

"You got any brothers and sisters?"

He cracked a wise-guy grin. "Here and there. The old man's always drunk but he ain't a gelding."

"How come nobody said different when whoever spoke up laid out the way you were scattered in those two trucks?"

"How 'different'?"

"Dan Pool was in the back of your truck."

"So what? Who cares about a little thing like that?"

"Little things make the difference more often than not. Was it just that none of you wanted to cooperate with a white man? A white detective? Was that it?"

"Sure. Why should we?"

"Or was it maybe that one of you wanted about as much confusion as he could get about who was where and when and who fired the first shot? Things like that?"

"What would that have to do with anything?"

"That's the way an innocent man would think. But you take a guilty man, now. He tends to start thinking about every little thing, every blade of grass, every speck of dust, until he starts believing everything he ever did could look suspicious. So he lays the groundwork for an elaborate alibi every chance he gets. That's usually what trips him up. Not one big lie but a whole bunch of little lies about things that don't really mean a thing."

"Well, who're you saying's guilty?"

"I'm not saying any particular person is guilty of anything, Willy. What I'm talking about is the way guilty men in general act a lot of the time."

"That's a lot of Bull Durham. Who the hell you think you're kidding?"

"Let me ask you, Willy, before you start trying to weave a web of lies like a guilty man. Where'd you get the idea that some passenger on the diner raised his glass to you?"

"I saw it."

"No you didn't, Willy. I checked it out and you couldn't see a thing like that from the distance you claimed you were. Not even if you had the eyes of a hawk. So, if you're telling the truth about seeing such a thing, then I've got to believe you weren't even in the truck but ambushed down in some gully or fold of land maybe forty, fifty, no more than a hundred yards away. Laying on your belly with a scoped rifle and some cupronickel bullets with crosses cut in their noses—"

"I was in the truck!"

"So where did you get the notion about the fella raising his glass?"

"I don't know. I heard it someplace."

"In the Silver Saddle Saloon after you did like Dan Pool told you and went inside for your last beer of the night?"

He was thinking about it. It was slow going, and I wasn't going to give him time to sort it out how he could save his skin without dumping one of his pals in the stew.

"How about right after Dan Pool came back in from talking to his lady friend?" I said soft and easy, like it was his own head talking to him.

His eyes remembered and he started to nod, then caught himself. "I can't remember. How do you expect me to remember a little thing like that? Maybe I just thought I saw it. Maybe I just made it up."

"I'll just have to find out, won't I?" I said.

Thirty-one

IT WAS ONLY WHEN I finally came face to face with Dan Pool in Des Moines that I realized I'd never seen anything but the back of him. He wasn't that impressive, just sullen and mean, his young face all worn away and gouged by hard living.

He was all alone in a cell, sitting there like he'd burst into flame any minute.

"You remember me?" I said.

"Never laid eyes on you," he snapped back.

"Well, come to think of it, I never laid eyes on you, either. All I ever saw of you was your back."

"That's all I ever want to see of yours, buddy, so why don't you take a walk?"

"Aren't you starting to wonder?"

He wanted to be sullen and surly but he couldn't help a natural curiosity.

"Wonder about what?"

"Wonder about how come you're sitting here holding the bag while the rest of your war party are out walking free."

"Who says so?"

"Well, you stood right there and heard the judge tell Woodman he could walk out on his own recognizance, didn't you? Willy and Charlie are out in Jim Willows' custody. So are Rider and Calgary. What do you think's going on?"

"I don't know what's going on. What do you think's going on?"

"Maybe it's got something to do with your lady friend."

"What lady friend?"

"The one in the green Cadillac with the red pin-striping."

He stared at me for a long minute.

"Who told you about that?"

"It's common knowledge by now. You think the cops are sitting on their hands? They know about the woman. They know about the car. Pretty soon they'll know the name."

I let him think about that.

"Okay, you want to see my back, here's my back," I said, and turned around like I was ready to leave.

"Give me a goddamn minute to figure this out," he said.

"What's to figure out? You can look at it two ways. Somebody's seeing to it you take the fall all by yourself so they can dump you in the animal house where some paid killer'll walk up behind you one day, one night, and put a shank into your liver."

"What's the other way?"

"You might get the shank right in here. Or maybe they'll hang you instead."

"What the hell's going on here? I didn't do anything. I didn't even fire my rifle at the goddamn train. I shot into the air."

"Well, now, wait a minute. You did *something.* This isn't happening to you because you were at the movies or a rib joint having a beer."

"It wasn't even me she came to first."

"It was Abe Woodman, was it?"

He looked at me like he was a little surprised and a lot relieved. Every time I fed him a little something I figured out *could* have happened, he thought I knew one hell of a lot more than I knew and it made it easier for him to give up and open up.

"Abe turned her down, right?" I went on.

"He don't like to take many chances. I told him there wasn't much of a chance to take doing what she wanted him to do."

"All she wanted him to do was drive a pickup for a couple of miles alongside the California Zephyr going west? All she wanted him to do was fire a couple of shots in its general direction?"

"That's right."

"Why? Did she give him a reason for engaging in such foolishness?"

"Just a joke. Just hoo-rahing a friend of hers on the train who was always complaining about modern times, how the old Wild West was dead and gone."

"Now, you didn't really believe that horse pucky," I said, giving him the one-eye.

He looked at me without blinking. "That's what she said. That's what I believed."

"How much was she offering?"

"Two hundred bucks."

"So you contacted her and said you'd arrange it."

"I did better than that. I convinced Abe to go along. The way I set it up with six of us in two trucks, if there was any complaints they'd have a hell of a time pinning the blame on any one of us."

"Why'd you meet her at the Silver Saddle?"

"She said she wouldn't pay me until she knew for sure I did what I said I'd do."

"How'd she know if you did or not?"

"She said she'd be out there watching."

"So she paid you off?"

"That's right."

"She make any other promises?"

"She said, if anything was to happen where we got in any trouble, she'd see to it that it didn't come to anything."

"And you believed her?"

"I guess I didn't give a damn if she could or not."

"But you've changed your mind?"

"I guess."

"So give me a name."

"She never gave me one."

"You take care of yourself the next day or two. I'm going to see if I can get you out of the cage."

When I went out to turn in my visitor's badge, the clerk handed me a note. "This man said to call as soon as you got the chance."

I looked at the number. It was George McGilvray's.

I called him at his office and he picked up himself.

"I was just ready to call you and ask a favor," I said.

"Is the favor you were going to ask that I should call around, check my police contacts, my legal contacts, my contacts in the Iowa state attorney's office and see who's dealing these Indians out here and there like a hand of cards?"

"Something like that."

"There's no conspiracy. No pressure's been applied, no favors asked, no old debts called in. The youngsters were separated for obvious reasons. Likewise Rider and Calgary. Bureau of Indian Affairs could step into their cases and they did. That leaves this Woodman and this Pool."

"How come they let Woodman walk and kept Dan Pool?"

"Because Dan Pool's got some priors. Simple as that. That's what I was told."

"Wait a minute, I thought you said there was no conspiracy."

"That's the way it's supposed to look. But my nose and my belly tells me somebody's making the puppet dance. I can't point a finger or name a name, however, so me sharing your suspicions doesn't help you, right?"

"The way it *looked* already helped me. I wove a tale for Dan Pool based on what we suspected and he decided to cooperate."

"Was it murder?"

"Yes."

"You know who did it?"

"Marla Kassabian, the mistress."

Thirty-two

"I DIDN'T TRUST HIM to watch out for me anymore. He said he'd take care of me. I knew I had to take care of myself," Marla Kassabian said, sitting there in a green robe in her cool green living room.

"You'll have to explain that to me. I don't know how killing him gave you any security."

"He wanted to sell up. The shares I'd collected from him over the years were like an annuity for me."

"You'd still have them. You'd still have a piece of Chaney Enterprises no matter who owned the company."

She shook her head. "I had the income from them and they'd be willed to me after his death, but while he was alive Harry had control of them. He needed them to throw into the fight in case Lewis Warden and Florence fought the take-over bid by the Whente Corporation."

"He'd have paid you for them."

"Perhaps he would have, perhaps not. Even so, I didn't want to chance it."

"So you killed him to protect your holdings?"

"Yes, that's right."

I let it go for a minute.

"How did you come to hire Dan Pool?"

"I met him through Abraham Woodman."

"How did you meet Woodman, then?"

"Nothing exotic. Nothing sinister."

"No, I didn't think so."

"I have an elderly cousin lives in Cedar Rapids," she said. "I try to visit her now and then. Every three months or so. She wanted to go to the bingo games at the Mesquakie Settlement. It's about sixty miles and she doesn't drive anymore. I went with her and Abe noticed me."

"I'm sure you would've caught his eye."

"Yes, in that gathering, I caught his eye."

"He seems like a nice young man."

"He is. Very outgoing. Very friendly. But very solitary really. Much alone."

Like yourself, I thought.

"You saw him after that?"

"Oh yes," she said, and looked at me as though asking me not to go too far asking questions about her and Abe Woodman.

"Must have been difficult, you living in Denver," I said.

She shrugged. Who cared about that when there was a young man waiting.

"Did you ask Abe Woodman to murder Harold Chaney?"

"No!" she yipped. Then she settled back down again and said, "He never knew what I had in mind."

"You sure? You think he believed that story you

gave him that all you were doing was playing a joke on somebody?"

"Probably not."

"Dan Pool sure didn't believe it."

"Dan Pool didn't care one way or another. He saw a chance to make a couple of hundred dollars with practically no risk."

"A man was going to end up shot in the head—"

"He didn't *know* that. If they got caught, he could always say he had no idea anyone was going to get hurt, let alone killed."

"That wouldn't help him much. He'd still be an accessory."

"Along with all the rest. One of the pack."

"The police could've finally singled him out just like I did."

She smiled briefly. "Then he could have made a bargain and sold me for his own immunity."

"So you took all these chances just for money," I said, letting the doubt show in my voice and attitude.

We sat there in the quiet. The ticking clock started getting loud. I watched her bosom, neck, and face color up like a fire was burning beneath the skin. I watched the tears cover her eyes like a mist and her mouth start to tremble with hurt and rage.

"Harry had this thing for redheaded women. Did I tell you?" Her voice was soft and under tight control.

"Pip?"

"His new love's name is Elizabeth, too. Just like his first wife's."

The ticking clock got loud again.

"Do you know what that fool did?" she said, finally breaking the silence. "He showed me the emerald. He asked me what I thought of its quality. I know a lot about emeralds. They're my favorite gemstone." She touched her hair. "He claimed it was a gift for his wife. Emeralds are all wrong for a woman with Florence's coloring."

"Did you see the inscription inside the band?"

"No, I didn't see it. I just saw the loose stone. I found out about Elizabeth Shanahan after I saw it."

"There's a Shanahan works for a legal firm . . ."

"Phil Shanahan. Elizabeth's his daughter. That's how Harry and she met, through her father, through business."

That damned clock wouldn't shut up.

"Maybe he was trying to reach back for his youth," I said.

"What youth was I going to reach back for? He'd taken it."

It sounded dramatic, his stealing her youth. It drew your sympathy. You could see how this villainous man had ruined a good and loyal woman's life, just tossing her aside like an old shoe. But, behind it all, was the fact that she'd negotiated a deal that allowed her to live better than most. Nobody'd twisted her arm. She hadn't deprived herself. Not even when it came to taking young lovers like Abe Woodman. I wasn't making judgments. I wasn't judging her. I wasn't judging him, either. Even so, it was hard not to feel sorry.

"Now! Having confessed all that," she said, slapping her knees as though ready to have a party, "why don't we have a drink and talk about something else?"

"I'm afraid we've got things to do."

"Like what?"

"Like calling the police."

She started laughing then, just like she'd laughed that one time when we both got the joke at the same time, only not quite so genuine.

"Jake, for heaven's sake, if you try to peddle this to

the authorities, if you try to claim I admitted a word of it, I'll just deny it."

"You just confessed to an officer of the law."

"To a railroad detective."

She went to make the drinks.

"Besides," she said, "you didn't Mirandize me. Would you like to Mirandize me?"

Thirty-three

So Marla Kassabian was still as free as a lark, walking around in her green dresses, driving around in her green car with the red pinstripe, red hair flying.

And I still had to find a way to make a case against her or haunt her till she made a mistake and gave herself away.

I called up Marcus Sears to find out if the will had been read or was going to be read. He knew the time and place and told me after only a moment's hesitation.

I'd always known that Sears had a lot of close friends in the financial community, and I suppose it should have come as no surprise to me that he was close enough to Harold Chaney to appear at the funeral, but it wasn't until I saw the way he'd interacted with Jessica Chaney at the funeral home that I realized the relationship went beyond business.

He asked me if I intended to attend the reading and when I said I did he made no comment.

So it was back to Chicago again for me.

At first the receptionist at the Malcolm, Seagrave, Morrison, and Hedrick offices in Chicago didn't want to let me in. I asked her if Phil Shanahan was back from Marshalltown and she said he was inside Hedrick's office with the others.

"Other what?"

"Other persons concerned with the reading of the will."

"Do me a favor, would you?" I said. "Buzz on through and ask Mr. Shanahan to come on out here for a minute. Tell him it's his old friend, Jake Hatch, from the Burlington Northern."

She hesitated so long I finally had to show her my badge.

When Shanahan came out of Hedrick's office he was all smiles, but there was a funny look around the eyes.

"What are you doing here, Mr. Hatch?"

"Isn't it Jake and Phil anymore?" I asked.

"Sure, Jake, what can I do for you?"

"You can tell this young lady that I'm allowed inside for the reading of the will."

"Well, that's not exactly true, is it?"

"It'll soon be a matter of public record and I see no reason why I shouldn't sit in as the representative of a possible litigant in some future action."

"How do you make that out?"

"If any or all of the family—mother, wife, daughter and/or son—brings suit against the Burlington Northern for the loss of support or comfort from son, husband, or father, I think it only fair and proper that the Burlington Northern should have an idea of how Harold Chaney distributed his estate, thereby assigning the measure of loss incurred by each of them."

"But, as you say, it's soon to be a matter of public record."

"I'd just like to get a head start. Show the front office Jake Hatch is not the sort of man to let any moss grow on him."

"I'm afraid I couldn't take it on myself to let you sit in."

I was looking for another way to make my case when Marcus Sears walked in, escorting a woman in a mink coat.

For a second I thought it was Marla Kassabian, and then I saw that the lady was twenty years younger.

Shanahan went over to kiss his daughter as Sears stepped away with the air of an aristocrat handing a princess over to a peasant.

"How are you, Jake?" he said.

"You get around, don't you, Marcus?"

"Well, I have a lot of friends."

Shanahan had taken his daughter into the office with his arm around her, his head in close to hers, conferring about something he didn't want anyone else to hear.

Nobody had introduced me to her.

I moved Sears farther away from the receptionist's desk, wanting a little privacy of my own.

"Is she the reason why you tipped me the question about the weeping redhead at the funeral parlor?"

"I was hoping you wouldn't find her and question her. She was taking the loss very badly."

"Loss of what?"

"That's unkind, Jake. It's not like you to be unkind."

"And it's not like you to give me half a loaf, Marcus. Every time I've come to you before, you've either told me everything you thought could be useful to me or refused to tell me anything at all. How come you didn't mention that Chaney was taking on another mistress?"

"He was taking on a whole new life. He was going to

ask for a divorce as soon as the take-over was through. He was going to provide for Florence and the children. There was to be generous extra compensation for Marla Kassabian as well. Then he meant to marry Elizabeth Shanahan."

"Pip."

"Yes, Pip. That's what he called her."

"Because he called his dead first wife Pip?"

"Yes, he did, didn't he?"

"Jesus Christ, Marcus."

"A man's entitled to take what happiness where and when he finds it."

"So you were being a friend keeping it quiet?"

"I'd have done the same for any friend who asked for confidentiality."

"Was his intention to pretend to resist the take-over while surrendering to it confidential too?"

Sears drew himself up, dignified and only slightly offended, as only a man of his age and stature can do. "You can check the trades, Jake. I never used the information to benefit myself."

"Sorry. It was just a thought."

He forgave me as quick as he'd taken offense. He smiled.

"All's well. At my time of life, I can't afford to lose an old friend over so small a matter."

"At my time of life too," I said.

"We'd better get inside," he said, taking my arm.

Walking in with Marcus Sears that way, it seemed that everybody forgot I wasn't invited. Sears let go of me and went to sit in the client's chair on the right-hand side of Jack Hedrick's desk.

Hedrick half got up to shake his hand and then looked around to see if everyone was finally assembled as I quietly took a seat at the back of the room.

Marla Kassabian was sitting in the first chair in front of Jack Hedrick's desk on the left, the right front being reserved for members of the family—old Mrs. Chaney, Florence Chaney, Mark, and Elizabeth—who were most likely to be the beneficiaries of the will that was about to be read.

Lewis Warden was sitting with them.

Shanahan was sitting with his daughter Elizabeth in a sort of never-never land midway between the mistress and the wife, but further back.

There were ten or twelve men and women sitting toward the back of the room. I assumed they were long-time associates and employees who were going to benefit.

Jack Hedrick picked up the will, which was stapled inside pale blue covers, cleared his throat, and asked for a stipulation, for reason of expediency, that the boiler plate—"being of sound mind and body, etc." —was properly drawn.

He smiled as though they'd given him a compliment for good work when everybody who thought they had a right to assent murmured that assent.

Just like I figured, the little crowd in the back were all named and rewarded for service to Chaney and the corporation in varying degrees.

Personal keepsakes were bestowed, Lewis Warden being rewarded with a matched set of silver-mounted shotguns, which he'd apparently admired and coveted.

Provision had already been made for old Mrs. Chaney and the children through trusts and endowments. There were additional gifts more sentimental than valuable.

Florence Chaney was left house and furnishings, cars and vacation homes, securities and cash, a carefully proportioned share of Chaney's wealth that would withstand any attempt she might make to claim undue influence on anyone's part or cruel prejudice on her husband's.

Everybody was holding their breath, because the two redheads, the old mistress and the new, had not yet been named.

The beneficiary of the residual of an estate—often the lion's share—is left for last.

Already I could see Florence Chaney struggling with the humiliation she might soon have to suffer when her husband's interest in other women, his preference for them over her, would finally be made public.

"To Marla Kassabian, loyal friend and associate, I leave the condominium in which she currently resides, free and clear."

I could see the color flood her face. It wasn't bad, a condominium worth maybe four hundred thousand, but it was easy to see it wasn't as much as she expected or thought she deserved. She made a move, as though she wanted to get up and get out of there, but there was one more player in the game and she had to hear it all.

"To Elizabeth Shanahan (no mention of their relationship), the residual of my estate."

There was a gasp from Florence Chaney, quickly suppressed.

Marla Kassabian turned her head sharply, seeking out somebody. Her eyes landed on Elizabeth Shanahan, then quickly moved to Phil Shanahan. There was a smile of triumph on her lips and a look in her eyes like she was saying, I did my part, now you do yours.

I finally knew who'd killed Harold Chaney.

Thirty-four

It happens that way sometimes. You get a notion about a crime, or what could be a crime. You start looking over the cast of characters. Naturally the players at the front of the stage look clearest and best, the most likely suspects, the most probable thieves or killers.

Also, you take a look at the feature actors moving around right behind the principals.

While you're all wrapped up doing that, there are a couple of characters slipping around in the shadows at the back of the stage. A second cousin of the heroine, twice removed. An under-gardener. The butler. The family lawyer.

I sat there as Jack Hedrick wrapped up the proceedings, waiting for my chance.

When I was a youngster, I once worked a summer on an uncle's ranch up in the Dakotas, herding cattle, cutting the young ones out for branding. I couldn't figure out how those calves seemed to know what I was trying to do and how easy they slipped away from me. I was older than they were—though not by much—and I just couldn't figure out how they'd gotten so smart so young.

It was only later that I learned it was just the survival instinct of a hunted animal at work.

It operates with people too.

I don't know exactly the moment he knew that I knew, but right after Marla looked at him, Shanahan looked at her and then turned around and looked right at me, knowing I knew that he knew that I knew.

I hoped he wasn't going to run.

Everybody started leaving, going out in little groups, careful not to mix in with anyone from an unfriendly camp.

Marcus Sears, Phil Shanahan, and his daughter Elizabeth were last. At the elevators, Shanahan murmured into his daughter's ear, shook Sears's hand, and walked back to me.

"Suppose we get a glass of ale or a short whiskey?" he said.

"There's a place just around the corner," I said.

"The closer the better. That was dry work."

I didn't say anything.

Sears and Elizabeth were gone. We waited for the next elevator.

A couple of minutes later we were in the cocktail lounge. Shanahan ordered his boilermaker. I had a beer.

"Your daughter's going to be a very rich woman," I said.

"Yes. Yes, she is." He acted kind of vague, as though his mind was going like hell working something over while his mouth was on automatic. I could see it was hard going. The man was tired, exhausted with life. He tossed back the whiskey and quickly took a swallow of beer.

"That why you killed Chaney, so she could get to the bulk of the money quicker?" I asked.

He stared at me as though I'd slipped the rails.

"Greed. Of course. That's always considered the most powerful motive for murder, isn't it?" he said.

"I've always found that money usually figures into murder somewhere, somehow."

He drained what was left in his glass of beer, turned around, caught the waitress's eye, and, after he saw I'd had no more than a swallow of mine, ordered another boilermaker for himself.

"Elizabeth looks almost exactly like her mother did at that age," he said, in that funny voice people get when they start talking about the past and what might have been. "Beautiful girls, both of them. My wife was a lot smarter and more determined than Elizabeth, though.

"When she met and married me, she was the spoiled daughter of a well-off county family. They didn't approve her taking up with a common Irishman whose only interest and occupation was horses. She was determined to make something of me. She made me get an education and even chose my profession for me.

"Well, maybe you can make a lawyer out of an Irish horse trader, but you can't really make a silk purse out of a sow's ear. The day I got my wig should have proved something to her family, but they wouldn't even attend the ceremony.

"That was the bitter pill that spoiled it all. I didn't give a damn. She was enough for me. And after the baby came . . ." He downed the shot and almost lost it, choking and coughing for a minute, then recovering himself, wiping off his red face with a handkerchief. Swiping at his eyes, as well. "My wife couldn't manage it. She missed her family and her county friends. There were advantages she wanted for young Beth.

Social advantages they wouldn't let me buy or earn. When she left me, it seemed only natural that she should take the child, though it tore my heart."

He fell into a melancholy silence. When it looked like he wasn't going to go on, I said, "Is that when you came to the States?"

"I think I had dreams of making a great success and sending for them, bringing them here where all that snobbery and tradition couldn't affect us anymore. Foolish."

"Well, you had to try."

"You shouldn't try when there's no good in trying. It just makes you miss other opportunities. As it was, after a while, I didn't think of England or my wife or my daughter very often."

A lot of what he was saying was the truth and a lot of the feelings genuine but, the way these stories go, a lot was nothing but crocodile tears and whiskey.

"How is it that Elizabeth's with you now?" I asked, trying to nudge him forward.

"Her mother died two years ago. Elizabeth wrote to me, saying she wanted to come to me. I was overwhelmed. When I met her at the airport, though I'd not seen her or had a photo of her in years, I could have picked her out of a crowd of ten million. She was exactly like her mother. For a moment, as she walked toward me, not recognizing me, of course—though I *had* sent a photo so she would know me—I was twenty again. Just like that." He was acting almost bashful about what he was saying. "The Irish have always believed in magic."

I wanted to get back on track, to pull Shanahan back from his dreaming.

"Being a member of the law firm that handled Chaney's affairs, you knew that he'd made a new will, leaving the bulk of his fortune to your daughter. You trying to tell me you didn't shoot Chaney to get your hands on the money?" I said, trying to make it as harsh and blunt as I knew how.

He finished off his second beer.

"I shot Chaney because he was stealing my Elizabeth away from me. He was stealing my chance at a new life from me. He was an old man, older than I, and he was stealing my youth."

The waitress had been keeping a close eye on our table—business at that hour being slow and knowing a drinker when she saw one—and was over asking if Shanahan wanted another the second he set down his empty beer glass.

"Yes, one more time, my dear. A beer and a whiskey. My friend's a bit slow, but bring him a fresh beer as well. That one's gone flat."

When the waitress went away I asked him if he knew why Marla Kassabian had been willing to let me think she was the one who killed Chaney.

"What could you have done about it if she had?"

"You trying to tell me she just thought she'd have a little fun with the old railroad bull? Let him think he'd figured out a murder just for the few giggles it might give her?"

"Perhaps it was because I offered her a share of Elizabeth's inheritance in the event that the bulk of Chaney's fortune was left to Elizabeth."

"Why would Elizabeth do that and why would Marla believe she'd do that?"

"I made the argument to my daughter that Mrs. Kassabian had given a good many years to Harold Chaney. Far more than she had. My daughter's not a greedy child. She wasn't with Chaney for the money in the first place."

"So what you did is practically admit to Marla Kassabian that you had a hand in Chaney's death."

"She'd come to see me after she'd found out about Elizabeth and Chaney. I don't know what she hoped to accomplish. Perhaps she thought I didn't know about the affair and would've done something to stop it. Distraught women—discarded women—do all sorts of things in hope and desperation. I explained to her that I didn't like the arrangement but, since I knew my daughter so little, I could scarcely play the disapproving father."

The waitress came back with his third boilermaker.

"But I offered her a way to do something about it. I told her how she could set up a scene that would scare the hell out of Chaney. Make him feel the cold hand of death brush by. Make him realize in a split second how much she meant to him and how foolish he'd be to give up his last few years in the comfortable arms of an old love for the doubtful pleasures of a young woman's arms. The day you realize you're close to it is the day you'll choose comfort over excitement every time."

"She didn't believe that fairy tale, did she?"

"Hell, no. She read my intention in my eyes, just like I was reading her willingness to help me kill him in hers."

"How'd she feel about setting up her little rodeo after I got onto her?"

"She came to me again. I told her you had no case. What was more important, you had no authority. I think she knew that all along. But she wanted something more from me. She said she'd even fortify your belief that she was the one who killed Chaney. For a price."

He smiled at me as though I was a schoolboy and he the teacher.

"You must've both been mighty sure I couldn't get the job done," I said.

"We were. What did you have against her? A bunch of wild surmises. A flimsy structure of speculations. And that's all you've got against me. You're just a railroad detective, Jake Hatch, and that's not important enough to bring down any indictments and open up any trials for murder." He downed the shot without difficulty and drank half the glass of beer.

"You've got me all wrong, Shanahan," I said. "I don't bring charges with nothing but wild surmises and flimsy speculations in my pocket. And when I make a claim about homicide there's any number of people who are ready to listen. When I go to the D.A. with what I've got, they'll be bringing down an indictment."

He was half-drunk and cocky. Or else he just didn't give a damn.

"What is it you've got?"

"Cupronickel."

"I beg your pardon."

"England's the only place where they plate bullets with cupronickel anymore."

"I never would have known that."

"Neither would I, except for a lady friend who knows all there is to know about guns and ammunition."

"Traces of cupronickel in the wound?"

"That's right."

"Shooting enthusiasts must trade ammunition all the time. A pocketful here, a pocketful there."

"We're talking about a pretty small group here, connected up one way or another."

"I grant you that, but the bullets could have come in from another source. A casual source. Couldn't they?"

I didn't say anything, just sat there looking at him as the waitress brought another boilermaker for him. On the house.

"Is that the way you're going to play it?" I finally asked.

"If any authority is foolish enough to act on such slender evidence, if any prosecutor is foolish enough to present such claptrap as cupronickel bullets in evidence, that's exactly the way I'm going to play it. You've got nothing, Jake. Not a trace of damning physical evidence. No chain of evidence linking me to the crime."

"I've got Marla Kassabian."

"And what would she testify to? That I convinced my daughter to give a little of a substantial fortune to an old, discarded mistress? That she read an intention in a drunk's eyes? That she went along with a silly charade? No, Jake, I'm afraid you'll get no help there. She won't link me to it. There's no way you can even place me close to the scene of the crime."

He smiled the way a man smiles when he knows he got away with something big, and saluted me, the man who lost the game, with his shot glass. So I smiled, and he saw something in my eyes. He hesitated half a beat, then downed the whiskey.

"There you go," I said. "There's how I'll put you on the scene. You can't go too long without a drink. There's going to be a bar, and a bartender who remembers you and your English accent, somewhere on the western skirt of Ottumwa."

Thirty-five

Bess and George McGilvray invited me to supper. I brought Maggie Wister along.

"Some little things are bothering me, Jake," Bess said, after the dishes had been cleared away and we were sitting having second cups of coffee.

"What's that?"

"How come that young Indian, Abe Woodman, hired that expensive lawyer firm?"

"He didn't. Marla Kassabian did. She wanted to protect him."

"Why didn't she do the same for Dan Pool?"

"She never had an affair with Dan Pool. She'd met Abe Woodman out at the reservation at the bingo game and they struck fire. Besides, she never actually hired the firm. Jack Shanahan said he'd represent Dan Pool on his own, without actually calling on them."

"Why would he do that? Why wouldn't he want to just stay out of it?"

"I thought I was making up a scary tale, telling Dan

Pool about how he was being isolated and set up for the kill in some jail. But that's what Shanahan really had in store for him. Dan Pool thought he was only dealing with Marla Kassabian. He made veiled threats when she met him at the Silver Saddle in Tama. She told Shanahan. Shanahan decided to take Dan Pool out."

"He was going to get another prisoner to kill him?"

"Lawyers have a hundred connections inside a dozen joints. It wouldn't have been hard to get somebody to do him the favor."

"Would you like some more coffee?" Bess asked.

When I said yes, Maggie motioned Bess to stay where she was and went to the stove to get the pot.

"I see a loose end, here and there," George said.

"Like what?"

"Like how come you never even bothered to question that man Terrence Pickering after Florence Chaney said he might be somebody who had it in for her husband?"

"That's easy. I had her figured for the killer at the time, and I thought she was just throwing sand in my eyes."

"That's a hell of a careless way to run an investigation."

"But there wasn't any investigation, George. I didn't have any jurisdiction. I didn't even have permission from the railroad."

Maggie had filled the cups of those who wanted more coffee and had put the pot down on a hot pad, freeing her hands so she could sign.

"All Jake was doing was nosing around," she said.

"Any other loose ends?" I asked George.

"If there is, I'm too tired to find them," he said.

"I'm feeling a little weary myself," I said. "I guess I'll drive Maggie home."

We got up and put on our coats. Maggie gathered up

Tippie. George walked me out to the car while Maggie and Bess tarried at the kitchen door. I could see our breath as we talked of small matters, the weather and the coming baseball season and the rising cost of living. I saw Maggie and Bess embrace. I remembered when I was a small boy waiting while my mother and father said good night to another husband and wife.

It seemed to me such a good thing, men and women living life in pairs.